A NEW CAMFIELD NOVEL OF LOVE BY

BARBARA CARTLAND

Born of Love

JOVE BOOKS, NEW YORK

BORN OF LOVE

A Jove Book / published by arrangement with
the author

PRINTING HISTORY
Jove edition / December 1992

ISBN: 0-515-11000-0

Jove Books are published by The Berkley Publishing Group,
200 Madison Avenue, New York, New York 10016.
The name "JOVE" and the "J" logo
are trademarks belonging to Jove Publications, Inc.

PRINTED IN THE UNITED STATES OF AMERICA

10 9 8 7 6 5 4 3 2 1

Born of Love

"Why do you not wish to marry me?" the *Duc* enquired.

"I should have thought the answer was obvious," Marcia replied. "I do not love you, and I can only ask you to make it quite clear to my Father that you have no wish to marry me."

The *Duc* stared at her.

He knew that any girl in the length and breadth of France would jump at the opportunity of marrying him.

It had never struck him for one moment that anyone on whom he even smiled would refuse him their favours.

Yet this young girl, who he admitted reluctantly was exceedingly beautiful, did not wish to be the Duchesse de Roux!

*A Camfield Novel of Love
by Barbara Cartland*

Camfield Place,
Hatfield
Hertfordshire,
England

Dearest Reader,

Camfield Novels of Love mark a very exciting era of my books with Jove. They have already published nearly two hundred of my titles since they became my first publisher in America, and now all my original paperback romances in the future will be published exclusively by them.

As you already know, Camfield Place in Hertfordshire is my home, which originally existed in 1275, but was rebuilt in 1867 by the grandfather of Beatrix Potter.

It was here in this lovely house, with the best view in the county, that she wrote *The Tale of Peter Rabbit*. Mr. McGregor's garden is exactly as she described it. The door in the wall that the fat little rabbit could not squeeze underneath and the goldfish pool where the white cat sat twitching its tail are still there.

I had Camfield Place blessed when I came here in 1950 and was so happy with my husband until he died, and now with my children and grandchildren, that I know the atmosphere is filled with love and we have all been very lucky.

It is easy here to write of love and I know you will enjoy the Camfield Novels of Love. Their plots are definitely exciting and the covers very romantic. They come to you, like all my books, with love.

Bless you,

CAMFIELD NOVELS OF LOVE

by Barbara Cartland

Author's Note

THE caves of the Dordogne were there for thousands of years before they were discovered.

One of the most important was found in 1868 and revealed, in addition to flints and carved bones of the Aurignacian Age, three skeletons of adults.

They were studied by Paul Broca, the Surgeon and Anthropologist who founded the School of Anthropology in France.

The discoveries in this cave, known as the Cro-Magnon, were of prime importance in prehistoric studies.

Some of the caves are exceptionally beautiful, with stalactites and stalagmites.

In 1901 a cave was discovered which demonstrated the importance of the Magdalenian Age at a time when all the Anthropologists were sceptical about prehistoric studies.

A secondary passage with cave drawings was the stage on which prehistoric man acted out his life.

This can be seen from the traces of domestic midden and the tools of the Magdalenian men, which have also been unearthed.

Later still, in 1940, the Lascaux Cave was held as one of the greatest prehistoric finds in Europe for the large number and life-like quality of the paintings on the walls.

This cave was discovered by four boys looking for their dog which had disappeared down a hole.

The majority of the animals which appear on the walls are female, and pregnant, symbolizing fertility—some appear to be transfixed by arrows.

The gorges for which the Dordogne is famous are so enormous that there are very likely to be a great many more hidden caves, which have yet to be discovered.

Born of Love

chapter one

1876

THE Dowagers sitting on slightly raised Divans at the end of the Ball-Room stiffened.

Then immediately their heads went towards one another, whispering.

Anyone watching them would have realised that Lady Marcia Woode had come into the room.

"Have you heard the latest?" one of the Dowagers murmured. "She rode along against Lord Ilchester's chestnut three times round Regent's Park."

"And she won!" another Dowager exclaimed. "It must have been a blow for Ilchester, who has grown far too big for his boots!"

"That is not the point," the first Dowager insisted. "She is behaving disgracefully, and I have made up my mind that I shall speak to her Father."

"I doubt if the Earl will listen," one of her friends retorted. "He adores Marcia, as an only child, and who can blame him? She is so beautiful!"

Several of the Dowagers sniffed.

At the same time, they could not deny that Lady Marcia was outstandingly lovely.

As she hesitated in the door-way as if looking for someone, candles in the huge crystal chandeliers picked out the gold of her hair.

They made her huge grey eyes shine like stars.

She was beautiful in a very different way from the *débutantes* who had preceded her.

In their first Season they were usually *gauche,* besides being shy and having nothing to say.

Lady Marcia had been brought up by her Father, the Earl of Grateswoode, to know how to express herself on any subject.

She was to be to him the son he had never had.

After Lady Marcia was born, it was impossible for the Countess to have any more children.

The Earl, therefore, had made the best of what, to him, was an exceedingly bad job.

He had treated Marcia almost from the time she could walk as if she were a boy.

She rode his most obstreperous horses; she shot with him over his huge Estate.

She took part, in fact, in every pursuit in which he was interested.

This, of course, included especially his horses, which were outstanding.

Lady Marcia's exploits with them had become the talk of London almost immediately after she had made her curtsy at Buckingham Palace.

When she rode in the Park, which she did early every morning, there was always a posse of men eager to escort her.

They were usually obliged to move with her in a body.

Then, to shake them off, she would laughingly ride ahead, galloping in what was considered an outrageous manner.

She would head towards the North side of the Park, which was not so fashionable.

Well-behaved young ladies rode quite slowly and never, it was emphasised, galloped.

There was no doubt that Lady Marcia, in this, her second London Season, was galloping in every way she pleased.

There appeared to be no-one able to control her.

She had paused for only a moment at the door-way of the Ball-Room.

A second later there were half a dozen men asking her to dance with them.

She deliberately prevaricated, teased them provocatively, and finally chose the Duke of Buckstead to be her partner.

There was a little sigh amongst the Dowagers as they watched them moving round the room.

"I suppose she intends to accept Buckstead," one of them said. "After all, she will hardly get a better chance."

"They say he is frantic about her," another one remarked, "like quite a number of other men. But she turns them all down."

"If she goes on like this, she will end up an old maid," another woman said spitefully.

No-one bothered to reply.

It was obvious that as long as Lady Marcia looked as lovely as she did tonight, there was no chance of her remaining unmarried for very long.

Ever since she had first appeared on the London scene, she had been the talk of the town.

It was not just her beauty, but the way she behaved.

She appeared to enjoy life in an almost outrageous fashion.

Every day she thought of something new and unusual to do and refused suitor after suitor for no good reason.

It was supposed that she must be expecting someone more important than the man who had just offered his hand, his heart, and, of course, his title!

Marcia's relations had long since given up expostulating with her or her Father.

It was quite obvious that neither of them listened.

As the Earl was the Head of the Family and an exceedingly wealthy man, the majority of his relations were dependent on him.

There was therefore little they could do.

Marcia danced round the room with the Duke until the music stopped.

Then, as several other couples did, they walked out of the long windows and into the garden.

The garden at Devonshire House had always been noted as a place for lovers.

It was said that more proposals had taken place under its trees than anywhere else in London.

It also served as a meeting-ground for many an *affaire de coeur*.

There was no doubt that tonight, at any rate, the air vibrated with love.

The trees were hung with Chinese lanterns and the paths were lined with little flickering fairy-lights.

Only where the garden sloped down the hill to Berkeley Square was there darkness except for the light of the moon.

Marcia moved over the soft green grass towards the fountain.

She was always fascinated by fountains.

She thought that the drops of water thrown up into the sky were like tiny prayers moving towards Heaven.

She was thinking of the fountain she had just persuaded her Father to install in the garden at home.

It would look beautiful surrounded by the hedges with their elaborate topiary work.

This was characteristic of the garden which had been laid out originally by the first Earl in the reign of Charles II.

"You have not given me an answer, Marcia," the Duke said almost sharply.

She had almost forgotten he was there, and his voice made her start.

"I am sorry, George," she answered. "I was not listening. What was your question?"

"The question I have asked you before and to which you have never given me a direct answer," the Duke retorted. "I want you to marry me. I know I could make you happy."

Marcia looked away from him towards the fountain.

The Cupid was holding a *cornucopia* in his arms from which water sprang.

There was the soft music of a dreamy Waltz coming from the Ball-Room.

It struck her that this was a very appropriate place for the Duke to propose.

Yet she knew she could not give him the answer he wanted.

"It is no use, George," she said. "You know I will never marry until I am in love, and I do not love you."

"Why do you not love me?" he asked in a truculent tone.

At twenty-eight he had been pursued by every ambitious Mama in the whole of the *Beau Ton*.

It seemed to him extraordinary that when he had finally made up his mind to marry he should receive a refusal.

How could this mere girl be apparently the only young woman in London who did not love him?

"The fact is," he said aloud, "you know nothing about love except what you have read in some rubbishy novelette or dreamt about when you were still at the age of enjoying fairy-tales."

"What is wrong with that?" Marcia asked.

"It is not practical," the Duke said. "You know as well as I do, Marcia, you will make a very beautiful and very much admired Duchess."

Marcia turned from her contemplation of the fountain to look at him.

"My husband would be the Duke," she said quietly.

"Well, what is wrong with that?" The Duke echoed her words.

He was well aware that he was spoken of not only as the most eligible bachelor in society, but also as the best-looking.

He had been painted by no fewer than three eminent artists.

The portraits were hung in Buckstead Castle for everyone to see.

"Let us talk of something else," Marcia said unexpectedly. "I thought your horse ran very well at Ascot yesterday. It was a pity it did not win."

"It was the jockey's fault," the Duke said angrily. "I have sacked him, and the next time I enter *Champion* in a race he will come in first."

Marcia smiled at the determination in his tone, and he added:

"And that is what I intend to do where you are concerned. We will have no more nonsense about it! You will marry me and we will announce our engagement next week."

"We will do nothing of the sort," Marcia declared. "I have told you, George, that while I like you as a friend, I have no wish to have you as my husband."

"Damn it!" the Duke swore. "You would try the patience of a Saint, and I refuse to take no as an answer!"

He put his arms round Marcia as he spoke.

She knew he intended to kiss her, not gently but fiercely and demandingly, as if he thought it was his right.

She did not struggle.

She just quickly moved a little, and in some way upset his balance.

His arms were already going round her, but his feet slipped.

As he fell sideways, he toppled over the stone bowl of the fountain into the water.

And as he fell he swore again.

Marcia did not stop either to listen or to see how wet he was.

She merely turned and walked away.

She disappeared among the trees, which would lead her back into the house by a different route from the one by which they had come.

Much later that evening Marcia was driving back with her Father in his comfortable carriage to their house in Grosvenor Square.

"What happened to Buckstead?" the Earl asked. "I saw you dancing with him soon after we arrived, and then he disappeared."

Marcia did not answer and after a moment the Earl said:

"Do not tell me that he asked you to marry him and you refused."

"He asked me for at least the sixth time, and yes, Papa, I refused."

The Earl made an exasperated sound.

"You refused Buckstead! But why? Good God, girl, you will never have a better offer. He is undoubtedly the richest Duke in England."

"You know the answer, Papa," Marcia said quietly.

The Earl was still feeling for words when the horses came to a standstill outside their house.

It was a very impressive building.

The Earl had had a great deal of redecorating done to it the previous year, before Marcia made her *début*.

He had thought, then, that it was unlikely that he would spend another Season in London.

It was quite obvious that with her beauty and her background, Marcia would be fêted and pursued.

Every eligible bachelor who felt the time had come when he must take a wife and settle down had proposed.

But her relations and the Society Dowagers were all stunned when she refused them one after another.

The Earl, however, had thought when Buckstead became interested that his daughter had been right in taking her time in choosing a husband.

Buckstead, as he had just said, was the richest Duke in England, and was also among the most important.

His wife would be by tradition appointed a Lady of the Bedchamber to Queen Victoria.

Buckstead himself was spoken of with respect by the Prime Minister and quite a number of other leading Statesmen.

What also pleased the Earl was that the Duke had a racing-stable as outstanding as his own.

He thought that between them they could produce horses which would enhance the already great reputation of English horse-flesh.

A footman hurried down the steps to open the carriage-door.

As the Earl got out he said:

"I want to speak to you, Marcia. So let us go into my Study."

She gave no answer.

She merely walked into the house and gave her evening-cloak to one of the footmen.

Then, after a somewhat wistful look at the staircase, she followed her Father across the Hall and down the passage to his Study.

It was a room that was entirely masculine.

When they were in London, Marcia had spent much of her time in it because it contained a great number of laden book-shelves.

At Woode Hall in the country there was a huge Library.

Marcia would, however, have felt deprived of something very essential if there had not been books for her to read wherever she was.

The candelabrum was still lit on the Earl's desk and the candles were alight on the mantelpiece.

As Marcia entered the room, the Butler waited in the door-way in case there were any orders.

"There is nothing else, thank you, Bowles," the Earl said.

"Good-night, M'Lord."

The Butler bowed before he shut the door.

Marcia gave a little yawn.

"It is too late, Papa," she said, "for one of your lectures. I know you are upset that I will not marry George, but there is nothing I can do about it."

"What do you mean, there is nothing you can do about it?" the Earl asked. "As I told you, you will never have a better offer, and his race-horses are out-standing."

"I agree with you," Marcia said. "But unfortunately I do not have to marry his horses, but him."

The Earl, who had sat down at his desk, brought his fist down with a bang.

"You are making a joke of it and, quite frankly, Marcia, it is nothing to joke about. You will have to marry someone. I am quite convinced that Buckstead will suit you."

"And I am quite convinced he will not," Marcia answered. "So what are we to do about it?"

"The whole thing is ridiculous," the Earl raged. "I let you refuse one offer after another, starting with a Viscount, when you were only just eighteen. I thought at the time that it was a mistake."

Marcia stood on tiptoe to look at her reflection in the mirror over the fire-place.

"I cannot understand, Papa, why you are in such a hurry to get rid of me. I am always so happy with you, and you know we have so many interests in common."

The Earl's expression softened.

"And I like having you with me," he said. "But you know perfectly well that you have to be married, and nothing will delight those evil-tongued old women more than to say that you are getting past your best and I am spoiling your chances by keeping you at home."

Marcia laughed, and it was a very pretty sound.

"Of course they will say that, Papa," she agreed. "But does it really matter? They are simply jealous because I am your daughter and are angry because you have never married again after Mama died."

There was a moment's silence before the Earl said:

"You know how much I miss your Mother. It would be impossible to find anyone to take her place."

"Yes, Papa, I know that. That is why I have tried to look after you as Mama would have liked me to do and to keep you amused. I can hardly do that and have a husband on my hands as well."

The Earl rose from his desk.

"You are twisting me round your little finger, as you always do. You know perfectly well that you have to be married, and it is normal, in Families like ours, for your Father to choose a husband for you and for you to accept that I am a better judge of men than you are."

Marcia laughed.

"Oh, Papa, you cannot bring up all that nonsense again. I have heard it all before. You agreed with me then that arranged marriages are uncivilised and the direct way to disaster."

"I did nothing of the sort," the Earl protested.

Marcia, however, went on:

"But because you loved Mama from the first moment you met, you promised that you would not force me to marry any man I did not like."

"I promised that within reason," the Earl conceded. "But now things have gone too far. You did not tell me that Buckstead had already proposed to you before.

Now I know about it, you will tell him that your answer is yes, and we will have no more arguments about it."

There was silence until Marcia, smiling a little wryly, said:

"I think it is unlikely that George will ask me again to be his wife after what happened this evening."

"What happened?" the Earl asked sharply.

"He tried to kiss me, saying somewhat unromantically that I would try the patience of a Saint."

"And so you would, but what happened?"

"I pushed him into the fountain."

"You did what?" the Earl exclaimed. "Good God, girl, do you always have to do something outrageous!"

"He should not have touched me. I had no wish for him to kiss me," Marcia said.

"Well, if he speaks to you again after being treated in such a manner, I shall be very much surprised," the Earl snapped.

"I did not actually mean to do it," Marcia confessed. "I was just protecting . . . myself against . . . him and his feet . . . slipped."

"I know exactly what happened," the Earl retorted. "You were using that damned Japanese ju-jitsu, which you insisted on learning. I knew it would end in trouble."

"But no-one is likely to know about it except you," Marcia protested. "It would be very undignified for poor George to have to confess that a woman had thrown him with a mere flick of her fingers. But I immediately disappeared, and if anyone saw him, they would merely have thought he had had too much to drink."

The Earl threw up his arms.

"You are hopeless, incorrigible! Heaven knows what I can do about you!"

Marcia moved a little nearer to him.

"Just accept me as I am, Papa."

"That is something I am not going to do," the Earl asserted. "In fact, now I think about it, I have a different solution to the whole problem."

"I doubt it," Marcia said. "And must I listen to it tonight? I want to go to bed."

"So do I," the Earl replied. "At the same time, you force my hand, and now you have to make the best of it."

"What do you mean by that?" Marcia enquired.

The Earl sat down in an armchair.

"I had a letter today from France which I found very interesting," he began. "In fact, there were two letters, but I did not really think of them in connection with you until just now, when you told me that you had insulted a young man of great importance and had refused to marry him. You have also made him a laughing-stock, which is something he will never forgive."

Marcia shrugged her shoulders.

"I have told you I am sorry. I did not actually make him fall into the fountain. But I had to protect myself."

The Earl drew in his breath as if he was trying to control his temper.

Then he said:

"Well, the damage is done and cannot be undone. What we have to do is to make excuses for your disappearance from the Social Scene, and that will be quite easy because of the two letters I have had from France."

"Whom were they from?" Marcia asked.

"The first," the Earl replied, "was from the *Duc* de Roux, inviting me to come over as soon as possible and see some horses which he thinks will interest me considerably."

Marcia realised now who her Father was talking about.

The *Duc* de Roux was known to have the best racing-stud in France.

She knew her Father had corresponded with the *Duc* for some time about their methods of breeding.

The two owners were due to discuss whether they should interchange stallions.

They were confident of producing horse-flesh which would be victorious both in France and England.

The *Duc* was, she remembered, vaguely related to her Father in that his Great-grandfather had married a member of the Roux Family.

She had never met the *Duc* but she had heard her Father often talk about him.

The Earl had been a friend of the *Duc*'s Father, who had stayed for Shooting Parties at Woode Hall when she was a child.

She wondered how this concerned herself, but she accepted that a visit to France under the circumstances would be a wise move.

"The other letter I received," the Earl was saying, "was from the *Duc*'s aunt, the *Comtesse* de Soissons, who I think I remember telling you was a friend of your Mother's when they were girls together and whom I saw last year when she came to England."

"Yes, of course, Papa," Marcia answered. "I remember your talking about the *Comtesse* and saying how charming she was."

"She tells me in her letter," the Earl said, "that she is very worried about her nephew, the *Duc*, in respect of certain matters that she does not wish to put on paper but will tell me when we meet. She is longing for him to settle down and get married."

Marcia gave a little exclamation of amazement, but did not interrupt.

"Unfortunately," her Father went on, "that is something he refuses to do, and consequently the Roux Family are in despair that he may not leave a son to inherit his Title, which would then die out altogether."

Listening, Marcia felt herself stiffen.

She had a perceptive feeling of what she was about to hear.

"I have therefore decided," the Earl said firmly, "although it may seem rather sudden, that, as the English Aristocracy is apparently not good enough for you, you will marry the *Duc* de Roux."

Marcia stared at him.

"But you just said, Papa, that he vowed to marry no-one."

"That is more or less what you also have decided," the Earl replied, "so we shall have to make both of you tiresome, obstinate creatures change your minds."

Marcia stared at him, and then suddenly she laughed.

"Oh, Papa, I have never heard anything so ridiculous! How can you possibly concoct a plot that could only come out of a magazine and expect it to be fulfilled in real life?"

"All I am prepared to answer," the Earl said heavily, "is that you have gone far enough in having your own way. I shall take you to France and force you to marry the *Duc* whether you like it or not."

"And supposing the *Duc* does not like it either?" Marcia asked almost jeeringly.

"I have a feeling, though I may be wrong," her Father replied, "that we can leave the *Duc* to his Aunt, the *Comtesse*. She is a very beautiful and very clever woman, and I suspect that between us we shall organise the most successful arranged marriage there has ever been."

Marcia got to her feet.

"I have never heard such nonsense in the whole of my life! I am sorry, Papa, I love you and I admire you, but you cannot force me up the aisle with a revolver pressed into my back."

She paused, but her Father was silent and she continued:

"I am quite certain the *Duc*, if he is anything like the Frenchmen I have heard and read about, will have a dozen Mistresses whom he will find far more alluring, far more exotic, and certainly far more sophisticated than I am."

The Earl spread out his hands.

"You know perfectly well that is not the way a properly brought up young lady should talk."

"It is your fault," Marcia retorted, "that I am not a properly brought up young lady! I have done all the things that you have done and enjoyed every minute of it. The truth is, Papa, that if I cannot find a man to love, it is entirely your fault, because no-one seems as attractive, as interesting, or as intelligent as you."

For a moment the Earl's eyes softened, and then he laughed.

"You little devil! You are trying to twist me, as you have always done, into getting your own way. But this time, my naughty daughter, you have gone too far! You know quite well that you cannot insult men like Buckstead without there being a tremendous scandal about it. You think nobody knows and nobody saw, but you may be sure that either he will talk or some Nosey-Parker was looking out of one of the windows."

Marcia had to admit to herself that this was very likely true.

"So what we have to do," the Earl calculated, "is to beat a quick retreat. There would be no better excuse than that I am going to France to see the *Duc*'s horses. If you are riding in the Park tomorrow morning, which I expect you will be, you will tell your admirers that you are leaving them for a time."

"Do you think they will believe that I want to see the horses as much as you do?"

"You must make them believe it," the Earl insisted. "Tell them too that you are invited to a Ball—there is certain to be one while we are in France—and we will also be attending several Race-Meetings. We will make sure we do all those things before we come home."

He paused to add:

"With, of course, the news that you are to marry the *Duc*."

"I think you are crazy, Papa," Marcia said. "Yet, at the same time, perhaps it would be wise for me to avoid the approaches of George, if he does speak to me again. It will undoubtedly cause a great deal of gossip if he does not."

"That is the only sensible thing you have said tonight," the Earl growled.

"I will think of a few more on our way to France, but let me make it quite clear, Papa, I have no intention of being married off to some French Duke who will be more interested in my Family Tree than in me as an individual."

The Earl would have argued, but she went on:

"He would prefer to spend his time enjoying himself with the *Courtesans* of Paris while I sit in the country amongst the turnips."

The Earl laughed as if he could not help himself.

"I cannot imagine your doing anything of the sort," he said. "At the same time, a *Duc* is always a *Duc,* and if Buckstead is not good enough for you, I can only hope that de Roux does not propose to you near a fountain."

Marcia walked to the Earl's chair and, bending down, kissed him on the cheek.

"I love you, Papa," she said. "However angry you may be with me, you never lose your sense of humour."

"I need it! The Lord knows how I need it!" the Earl snarled.

"Just think how bored you would be," Marcia said, "if I had married the Viscount or any of the other chinless young men who proposed to me in my first Season. You would have spent this year alone with a lot of old women clacking that you had to marry again."

"They can clack until they die!" the Earl declared. "But I have no intention of listening to them."

"And yet you expect me to listen to you," Marcia said softly.

The Earl reached out and took her hand in his.

"You are very lovely, my darling Daughter," he said, "and you know I love you and want your happiness. But quite frankly, you cannot go on as you are now. I have to play the heavy Father and find you some man

18

with whom you will be as happy as it is possible for us poor mortals to be."

"And that is not betting on a certainty," Marcia added.

She moved away from her Father to stand, once again, looking into the mirror over the fire-place.

"I suppose," she said, almost as if talking to herself, "that if I had been born plain, with a red nose and drab, mousy hair, I would be grateful to any man who would marry me because I am your daughter."

The Earl did not reply, although he was listening.

"Instead," Marcia went on, "because God has given me what people think is a beautiful face, and you, Papa, have given me an active and astute brain, I want more, so very, very much more, than just a man who will give me his name."

"A lot of men have offered you their hearts," the Earl said.

There was a pause and then Marcia answered:

"I know that. But what they have offered has not been good enough . . . not nearly . . . good . . . enough."

There was a note almost of despair in her voice as she turned and walked towards the door.

"Good-night, dearest Papa," she said. "Make plans for us to go to France, but remember, I do not promise to behave myself or to marry anyone unless he is the winner of the Grand Prix at Longchamps."

She opened the door as she spoke.

"After all," she added, "one of the Roman Emperors tried to marry his horse, so why not me?"

She shut the door before the Earl could reply, and he heard her foot-steps going down the passage.

He sighed and then, despite himself, he laughed.

"She is incorrigible," he said to the empty room.

Upstairs in her bed-room Marcia did not ring for her maid.

She had noticed before she went out that the woman had a cold, and had told her to go to bed.

"I'll be all right, Milady," the maid said.

"Go to bed and take a warm drink," Marcia had ordered. "If you are feeling rotten tomorrow, tell the Housekeeper that I said that you were to stay there."

She was glad now that she was alone.

She deftly managed to unbutton her gown at the back and threw it over a chair.

Then she walked to the window and drew back the curtains.

The stars seemed to fill the sky and the moon turned the roofs beneath her to silver.

She looked up at the sky.

She was thinking that because her name was a derivative of *Mars* she was part of the firmament just as the planet Mars was.

At night she felt as if she could fly up into the sky and leave the world and all its petty difficulties behind.

"What is wrong with me?" she asked. "Why do I not fall in love?"

She thought of the girls with whom she had made her *début* the previous year.

They had all giggled amongst themselves about the different men they fancied, and who fancied them.

Marcia had never wanted to giggle.

She would certainly never have betrayed a man by laughing at him behind his back.

She was not consciously aware of it, but her Father had taught her a Gentleman's code of behaviour.

She would never have discussed with another woman anything so intimate as a proposal of marriage, nor, as some girls did, read aloud the letters of love she had received.

Some had naturally been very intimate.

She was sorry that she had to hurt the writer by saying that she could not in any way reciprocate his feelings.

She was well aware that she had received more proposals of marriage than anyone else of her age.

Many were, as her Father had said, from men of importance and, like the Duke of Buckstead, the owners of a respected and ancient Title.

But what she felt for them was, she knew, a friendship, an interest, and, at times, some affection.

But it was not Love, not the Love which she sought.

She knew from the books she had read that men and women had fought for Love since the beginning of Time.

Sometimes they were lucky enough to find it.

"What is Love?" she asked the stars as she looked at them twinkling above her.

"How can I fall in love?" she enquired of the moon.

There was no answer.

Yet she could feel in the soft warmth of the air coming through the open window what she told herself were the vibrations of Love from the sky, the Love that lifted the heart and the soul.

It was Love that could transform what was ordinary and drab into something exquisite and beautiful.

Yet she had never found it.

She had, she admitted to herself, tried to believe herself in love, only to know it was just a pretence, not the sacred treasure she was seeking.

She knew that her Father was doing what he thought was his best for her.

She was not in the least angry that he intended to take her away with him.

He would try what she knew would be a fruitless task, to make her marry the *Duc* de Roux.

The only thing that made it amusing was to hear that the *Duc* himself was as reluctant as she was to be tied by the bonds of Matrimony!

For him a wife would be some-one with whom he would undoubtedly be bored in a few weeks!

For herself, she could not contemplate being touched and kissed by a man for whom she had no feeling except perhaps one of contempt.

'It will be a fruitless journey, but at least an interesting one,' she thought. 'I shall see France, which until now I have only read about in books, and I shall meet an important Frenchman who I am quite sure is as frivolous and pleasure-seeking as any *Casanove*.'

She could remember all too vividly the stories she had been told when she was young about the wild extravagance of the Second Empire.

Even her Mother had talked sometimes of the absurd behaviour of the rich men who spent fortunes on the grand *Courtesans* of Paris.

They bedecked them with jewels and provided them with houses, horses, and carriages.

They proclaimed themselves to be the most expensive and exotic women who had ever beguiled and bewitched the opposite sex.

'If that sort of thing,' Marcia thought, 'is still happening in Paris, then the *Duc* de Roux is not likely to notice me.'

She took one last look at the stars and pulled the curtains to.

As she got into bed she was not thinking of love or of the *Duc* de Roux.

She was wondering if his horses would be as exceptional as those belonging to her Father, to which so far she had never found an equal!

chapter two

THE *Duc* de Roux, riding back towards his *Château*, looked with satisfaction at his vines.

It was obvious that there was going to be a good harvest.

He knew that not only he but the people who had worked so hard on them would be delighted.

He was riding one of his superlative horses which he had bred himself and for which he was already a by-word in France.

But still he was not satisfied.

He wanted more and better race-horses, and he was quite certain that in that particular the Earl of Grateswoode could help him.

It was his dream that one day his horses would win not only in France but in England and in any country as thrilled by horse-flesh as he was.

On his last visit to Hungary he had learned a great deal he had not known before.

He thought it would certainly be an interesting subject to discuss with the Earl.

He looked ahead.

He could see his *Château* silhouetted against the dark trees that grew at the base of the huge rocks rising high against the sky.

Nowhere else in the world had he seen such a magnificent contrast between height and depth as in the Dordogne.

In other valleys, as in his, the vines had been planted which were to make for France one of the outstanding wines of Europe.

But the huge rocky gorges rising against the sky seemed aloof from anything human.

The *Duc* found himself almost believing that the peasants were right when they said that the gorges were inhabited by strange spirits.

He rode on and then started to climb from the flat ground of the valley up towards his *Château*.

As he drew nearer still to it, he could see the sparkle of the water from the fountains iridescent in the sunshine.

The beauty of his home had never ceased to thrill him.

He often went to Paris, and had travelled in other parts of the World.

But he always knew when he came home to the Dordogne that that was where he belonged.

Below the flight of steps which led up to the huge, porticoed front-door, a groom was waiting.

As he dismounted, the *Duc* said:

"*Aquilin* went very well today."

The groom smiled as if the *Duc* had paid him a particular compliment and led the horse away to the stables.

The *Duc* walked slowly up the steps and into the Grand-Hall.

There were four flunkeys in attendance, and he gave them his hat, his whip, and his gloves before the *Major Domo* said:

"*Monsieur le Comte* de Thiviers is in the *Petit Salon, Monsieur.*"

For a moment there was an expression of irritation in the *Duc*'s eyes.

He was not expecting his nephew, who was the son of his half-sister.

She was many years older than himself, being the only child of his Father's first marriage.

He had a suspicion as to why he had arrived at the *Château*.

However, there was nothing he could do about it, and he walked slowly towards the door to the *Petit Salon.*

He knew he would find his nephew, Sardos, waiting alone for him.

A flunkey opened the door, and as the *Duc* walked in, he saw he was right.

Sardos de Thiviers was alone, standing at the window with his back to the room.

He turned round quickly as he heard the *Duc* enter, and before his Uncle could speak, said:

"Good-morning. You may be surprised to see me, but I wanted to talk to you."

"It is certainly a surprise," the *Duc* replied. "Last time I heard of you, you were in Paris, and, I understand, having an extremely *amusing* time."

There was a note of criticism in the *Duc*'s voice, and an emphasis on the word *amusing* which his nephew did not miss.

Sardos de Thiviers was a good-looking young man.

His dark black hair was brushed back from his rather low forehead, and he was dressed in the very height of Fashion.

He was on the surface very prepossessing.

The *Duc*'s perceptive glance, however, noticed the dark lines of debauchery beneath his eyes which should not have been there at his age.

His thin lips could set in a hard line which was in strange contrast to the honeyed words with which he usually spoke.

Walking towards the fire-place which, as it was Summer, was filled with flowers, the *Duc* stood with his back to it, saying:

"I can guess why you have come to see me, Sardos. And my answer is the same as the last time you approached me. This cannot go on."

"I thought you might say that, Uncle Armond," the *Comte* answered. "But I have to tell you that I am in an extremely uncomfortable position which, unless it is rectified, will cause an unpleasant scandal."

The *Duc* stiffened, and there was a harsh note in his voice as he asked sharply:

"What is it this time?"

Sardos de Thiviers sat down in one of the armchairs.

"It was really not my fault, Uncle Armond," he began. "I did try to make some economies after you helped me last time, but I became involved with a man who swindled me out of a great deal of money and, as he is now bankrupt, there is no chance of my having it returned."

The *Duc* thought he had heard this story before, but aloud he said:

"On what else have you spent the quite considerable

28

sums that you received on your Father's death, besides the enormous amount of *francs* I gave you the last time you came here?"

The *Comte* did not answer, and after a moment the *Duc* said:

"I imagine that most of it has gone on women! Women, you must know by this time, exert the power of a magnet on any man's pocket, and quite frankly, you are not rich enough to afford them."

"That is not fair," Sardos de Thiviers complained. "You have had your fun, Uncle Armond, and there is surely no reason why I should not have mine."

"I certainly—had my fun—as you call it," the *Duc* replied, "but I could afford it better than you can. You have now gone too far."

"I do not know why you should say that," Sardos said angrily. "I am young and I want to enjoy life before I settle down, as my Mother urges, on that boring little Estate in Normandy where there is nothing to do and hardly a woman in sight who has not got one foot in the grave."

Just for a second there was a twinkle in the *Duc*'s eyes as if he was amused. Then he said:

"You have never tried to improve your Estate, which, after all, is yours, and you have bled your Mother of everything she possesses."

Sardos jumped up from the chair.

"Accusations, recriminations! Do I ever hear anything else?"

"You bring it on yourself," the *Duc* said severely. "You have spent an astronomical amount in the last few years. As I told you the last time I helped you, this cannot go on. You are not the only relative who is dependent on me."

"I know that," Sardos retorted. "But you are as rich as Croesus, and while they all batten on you, why should I be the exception to be left out in the cold?"

The *Duc* frowned.

"Hardly in the cold, Sardos. I was looking at the list only yesterday of the allowances I have made to my relations over the past three years, and you may be interested to know that you head it by a very large amount."

"I am your only nephew," Sardos said. "And my Mother is your only sister. Surely my claim is better than that of all those Aunts and Cousins who all cry 'Poverty, Poverty' the moment they see you."

"I would point out," the *Duc* replied, "that they are very grateful for what they received, and it ensures that they live in no more than reasonable comfort. Naturally they cannot throw money about in the way that you do on the prostitutes of Paris, who are notorious for their extravagance."

"No-one, of course, knows that better than you, Uncle Armond," Sardos de Thiviers said rudely.

But as he saw the expression on the *Duc*'s face, his tone changed.

"Please, Uncle Armond, please help me. I am in a dreadful mess and am being threatened by my Creditors. I cannot stave them off any longer."

The *Duc* did not answer.

He was thinking he had heard this plea many times before.

The words his nephew used were almost identical with those he had heard the time before, and the time before that.

"I promise," Sardos went on, "I promise on everything I hold sacred that I will not get into such debt

30

again. But help me, please, help me. This is the cry of a drowning man."

There was something over-dramatic, over-theatrical in the way he spoke which the *Duc* disliked.

Once again he remembered that his nephew had said the same thing in this same room the last time he had come to the *Château*.

The *Duc* glanced at the clock.

"I see," he said "that it is time for *déjeuner*. I therefore suggest we postpone this conversation until later in the day. I presume that you will be staying here, and suggest you sit down with my Secretary and make a list of everything you owe—stating in each case the sum and to whom it is due. Then we will discuss it and I will decide whether or not I will help you."

As he finished speaking he walked towards the door, and before his nephew could reply had left the room.

Alone, Sardos clenched his fists and stamped his feet.

"Curse him, curse him," he said beneath his breath. "Why the Hell cannot he give me the money and let me get on with it?"

He knew as he spoke that he hated his Uncle.

He wished he could reverse their positions and be able to tell the *Duc* how much he disliked everything to do with the Family.

Then he told himself that his only hope was somehow to persuade the *Duc* to finance him.

If that meant he would have to "eat humble-pie" and kiss his boots, then that was what he would do.

At the same time, he could feel his hatred of his own position sweeping over him like a Tidal Wave.

He had always been jealous of the importance of his Mother's Family.

While his Father had been undoubtedly an Aristo-crat, he could not compete with the magnificence and distinction of the *Duc* de Roux.

The Estate Sardos despised was in fact quite a pleas-ant one with distinct possibilities.

The ancient *Château* had been in the Thiviers Family for several generations.

It was, however, in a quiet and unfashionable part of Normandy.

From the moment Sardos had grown up, his one idea had been to get away and to enjoy himself in Paris.

A dashing young man was always welcome in the fast Parisian Society that was not accepted by members of the *Ancien Régime*.

Sardos was in his own way a success.

He was young and ardent, so women gave him their favours even though he could not pay as heavy a price as older and less attractive men.

Sardos longed to be important even if it was only among the women whom his Mother found unaccep-table and the men who would never have been invited to the *Château de Roux*.

It all proved very expensive.

When he could extract no more from his neglected land and dilapidated home, he was forced to approach the *Duc*.

"I hate him! I hate him!" Sardos told himself.

However, knowing that Luncheon would be ready, he walked down the passage towards the *Salon d'Or*.

It was where he knew the *Duc* and all the guests who were staying in the *Château* would have assembled before the meal was announced.

There was quite a collection of relatives who made every possible excuse to stay at the *Château*.

Nowhere else in France would they have been so comfortable.

Nor would the food have been so good, the wines so superb, and their Host so charming.

It infuriated Sardos that while he hated his Uncle, the rest of the Family fawned on him as if he were a King, if not a god.

They surrounded him now with, he thought, the expression of adoring spaniels on their faces.

They were listening to the *Duc* as if he had just dropped down from Olympus.

As he entered the *Salon,* the *Duc* said:

"We have another guest whom I think you were not expecting to see, and here he is."

Most of them naturally turned round and then exclaimed:

"Sardos! What a surprise!"

They were nearly all Aunts and Cousins.

The men, who were either husbands of his relatives or contemporaries of the *Duc,* looked at him, he thought, with contempt.

"I hate them too," he told himself.

Outwardly he was smiling with the charm he could switch on when it suited him.

It made the elderly of his female relatives invariably speak of him as "a delightful boy."

He paid the older women compliments.

He flirted with those who were younger.

By the time they went into the Dining-Room, everyone seemed to be in a good humour.

It was only the *Duc* who was watching Sardos somewhat carefully.

He was aware that he would try to extract money from some of his older relatives if there was a possibility of their having any to spare.

The food in the Great Banqueting-Hall, which could hold fifty or sixty guests with ease, was excellent.

The *Duc* was an epicure as well as a connoisseur, and he expected perfection in everything that concerned him.

Because in France everyone talked across the table as well as to their partners on either side, the conversation sparkled.

Sardos found himself being as witty and as entertaining as he could be in Paris.

The women there were skilled in drawing out a man to make him feel at his best.

Only when the meal was over and most of the guests had returned to the *Salon d'Or* did the *Duc* disappear.

He had some correspondence to attend to.

He also wanted to think about the problem of Sardos before he spoke to him again.

He did not go to the *Petit Salon,* where he often sat, but to the Library.

He thought Sardos would not follow him there.

He had a desk there which he used for his more formal affairs, also to compile the History of the Roux Family he when he had time.

The Family Tree was, in fact, laid out on the desk.

The *Duc* had been following it down through the ages, and as he sat down he saw at the bottom of it his own name.

Beside it there was the name of his wife—a wife who had married him and died the same year.

Although it had happened over nine years earlier, the *Duc* knew he would never forget it.

It had been an appalling disaster.

The *Duc*'s Father had, as was usual in aristocratic Families, decided when his only son, Armond, was quite young whom he should marry.

It had seemed to him a most admirable idea because his Estate and that of the *Marquis* de Lascaux marched side by side.

To join them would make the two families already the most important in the Dordogne even stronger than they were already.

The *Marquis*'s daughter, the *Duc*'s Father saw with satisfaction, was extremely pretty.

Although he had seen very little of her, he was quite certain she would prove the right wife for his son as soon as he was twenty-one.

It was usual in France for the Heirs to important Titles to be married as young as possible.

It was in the best tradition of their ancestors.

Armond grew up into an extremely attractive young man.

He was a brilliant equestrian and excelled as a swordsman.

He won a great many distinctions both at School and at University.

There was not a Family in France which would not have been thrilled to be united with the *Duc* de Roux.

He could have picked and chosen a daughter-in-law from any of them.

However, the *Duc* had made up his mind and given his word.

There was no question that Armond should marry anyone but her, who was literally "the girl next door."

The young people saw very little of each other because Armond was sowing his "wild oats" in Paris.

Also, he was already racing a few horses of his

own besides being tremendously interested in those belonging to his Father.

He shot and was outstanding at hunting wild boar.

He was invited to stay in almost every country in Europe by young Aristocrats of his own age who found him a delightful companion.

The marriage took place with all the pomp and ceremony that could be imagined.

An Archbishop and two Bishops took part in the Service.

His Holiness the Pope sent a special message to the Bride and Bridegroom from the Vatican.

The presents that the young couple received filled three rooms in the *Marquis*'s *Château*.

Armond looked amazingly handsome, and his Bride was beautiful.

Older women wiped away a tear as they drove away on their Honeymoon.

The showers of rose petals threatened to fill the Carriage.

It was after they had been alone together for two weeks that Armond faced the Truth.

His wife, so lovely to look at, was mad.

She was either vain, surly, and almost silent, or else she was screaming hysterically and quite unapproachable.

He was sensible enough to realise that he had been caught in a trap.

His wife's parents had been so eager to be allied with his Family.

They had therefore deliberately never let anyone have the least inkling of the Truth.

He realised when it was too late that he had practically never been alone with Cecilia.

When they were together he had always been suspicious that there was some-one listening at the door.

He knew now that it was not because Cecilia's parents had been afraid that he might frighten her, but that she might frighten him!

He took her back home.

He forced his Father and the *Marquis* to face the Truth.

Cecilia was taken to what was called a Hospital.

It was, in fact, an Asylum.

She died before she had been there a year, which was for everyone concerned a merciful release.

But it left Armond with a horror of Marriage, which made him swear that never again would he be trapped.

Never again would he allow anyone to arrange his life for him.

What actually happened was that Armond de Roux grew up and became a man.

He was only twenty-one and had been to all intents and purposes completely under his Father's thumb, not reluctantly or resentfully, for he genuinely loved and admired his Father.

He thought that the old *Duc* did, in fact, know what was best for him.

Now he told himself that he would be his own Master and that no-one should ever again interfere in his way of life.

Of course, it made him autocratic and what his Family thought was extremely obstinate.

But what it really was was a strong, overwhelming determination to do what he wanted, and not to be guided or pressured by anyone.

Of course, like all men, he tried to wipe away from his mind the horror of what had happened.

Naturally he went to the one Capital in the world which catered to a man who had been disillusioned.

Paris welcomed him with open arms.

He spent a brief period of time with the more alluring *Courtesans*.

But soon he discovered the beautiful and more exotic married women of his own Class.

They were only too ready to enjoy an *affaire de coeur* with the most handsome and exciting young man they had ever met.

To begin with, he sought the favours of women older than himself.

It was an education in the Art of Love in which the French excel.

It was an education for any young and ardent Romeo.

Then gradually, as he grew older, he became more fastidious, more difficult to please.

He found women of his own age but never those who were young or unsophisticated.

It was as if the ghost of Cecilia, her white veil trailing over her lovely face with its vacant eyes, haunted him.

Then his relatives began at first tentatively and then more insistently to beg him to produce an Heir.

But every word they spoke revived the horror of his Honeymoon as vividly as if it had happened only yesterday.

"I shall never marry until I fall in love," he told his Grandmother.

She looked at him in consternation.

"But, my dearest boy, what have you been doing all these years?"

"Enjoying myself, Grandmama," he replied. "That is not Love as I see it."

"I do not understand," she murmured.

Armond bent and kissed her cheeks.

"It would be a mistake for you to do so," he said. "But I promise you one thing, Grandmama, that when I do fall in love, I will bring my choice for you to approve."

The Dowager Duchess had to be content with that.

She loved her Grandson, and when she learned of his latest *affaire* with a beautiful Marchioness whose husband was frequently away, she had wept.

The Nurseries at the *Château* were closed.

She thought that by this time there should have been children playing round the fountains.

They would dip their tiny fingers into the stone basins to try to catch the goldfish.

"What can I say to him?" she asked when she prayed in the Chapel to her favourite Saint.

She knew, however, that Armond would not listen and would go his own way whatever anyone might say.

The *Duc* was meanwhile to all appearances extremely happy.

At the age of nearly thirty he was Monarch of all he surveyed, his Father having died over five years before.

He enjoyed introducing new methods to the Estate and had improved the Vineyards out of all recognition.

But his real delight was in his horses, which were becoming more and more successful year by year.

He won race after race until a number of other owners said sourly:

"If you go on like this, Roux, we shall have to emigrate if we want to win any races!"

The *Duc* laughed.

He knew that despite their jealousy and envy, he had already raised the standard of horse-racing in France.

He was sure that competition among those who had large Studs was the best thing that could happen.

Later that afternoon he went to the stables.

He usually visited his horses before they were shut up for the night.

He chose the one he intended to ride first thing next morning.

He talked to his Head Groom about one horse that seemed a little off-colour.

Then he congratulated the man on the performance of several others which he had in training.

As he walked back to the *Château* he realised that it was nearly half-past four.

The Earl of Grateswoode would be arriving at about that time.

Because he was a perfect Host, the *Duc* had remembered that as the Earl was English, he would like English Tea.

He had therefore ordered the Butler to serve it in the *Salon Bleu*.

His Chef had a predilection for making very elaborate *patisseries*.

He hoped he would not have forgotten what invariably appeared on the Tea Table in England—cucumber sandwiches.

'I want the Earl of Grateswoode to enjoy himself,' the *Duc* thought.

He walked into the *Château* by a side door and proceeded down the long corridor towards the front of the house.

It was fortunate that the Revolution had not given rise to much death or destruction in the Dordogne.

Much of the furniture in the *Château* was Louis XIV.

The *Duc* always remembered that a great amount of fine furniture and priceless paintings had crossed the Channel after the Revolution.

It was not only the collection at Buckingham Palace that was impressive.

There were five magnificent rooms at Scone Castle in Scotland, the Earl of Mansfield having been Ambassador to France at the time.

In fact, in almost every great house the *Duc* had visited he had found beautifully inlaid French *commodes* and boulle cabinets.

They could only have come from Versailles or from the *Châteaux* of the Aristocrats who had lost their lives.

The Roux collection had remained intact just as the members of the Family had kept their heads.

Yet many of their friends had lost theirs on the guillotine in the *Place de la Révolution* in Paris.

The *Duc* walked into the *Salon Bleu*.

There was no sign yet of the Earl, but another Visitor had arrived whom he had been looking forward to seeing.

She was very beautiful and had been acclaimed by all the great Artists in Paris as the most lovely woman of her period.

At twenty-five, the *Marquise* de Grozant was at the height of her beauty.

Her dark hair had blue lights in it, and it seemed as if her dark eyes had the same.

Her skin was very white and her figure perfect.

She was standing alone at the end of the room when the *Duc* entered.

For a moment he just stood still inside the door, taking in her beauty and her elegance which were somehow indescribable.

41

When she realised he was there, she went towards him with both her hands outstretched.

"I thought you had forgotten me," she said.

"Forgive me," he said. "I did not expect you so early."

He raised her hands one after the other to his lips, his mouth actually touching the softness of her skin.

And then, as he looked into her eyes, she asked:

"You have missed me?"

"Of course I have," he replied.

"Oh, Armond, I have been counting the hours until I could come here and be with you."

"And now you are here," he said. "I feel as if the sunshine has come with you."

It was a pretty speech.

She smiled at him, her red lips turning up to his.

Then, before either of them could move, the door opened and the *Comtesse* de Soissons came into the room.

"Oh, here you are, Armond," she exclaimed. "I was wondering where you were. I hear we have English Tea this afternoon."

"We have English Tea," the *Duc* said, "because my friend the Earl of Grateswoode is arriving. But let me introduce the *Marquise* de Grozant, who has just arrived."

The *Comtesse* held out her hand.

"I have heard about you, *Madame,*" she said. "The tales of your beauty have travelled even as far as the Dordogne."

The *Marquise* smiled.

"Thank you. It is a great delight to be here."

She looked directly at the *Duc* as she spoke.

He smiled at her, looking, although he did not realise

it, so handsome that it would be impossible for any woman not to be beguiled by him.

It was then that the *Major Domo* appeared in the door-way.

"The Earl of Grateswoode, *Monsieur le Duc,*" he announced.

The *Duc* gave an exclamation and walked towards the Earl.

As he held out his hand he realised he was accompanied by some-one else.

"How are you?" the Earl asked. "Thank you for the extremely comfortable Carriage you sent to meet us at the Station. I was, of course, extremely impressed by the speed with which it brought us here."

The *Duc* smiled and then, questioningly, his eyes went to the young woman standing beside the Earl.

"I hope you will forgive me," the Earl said, "but I have brought my daughter with me. I could not, as it happens, leave her behind in London. I felt sure you would find a small place for her somewhere in your large *Château.*"

As the train carried them from Paris to Southern France, Marcia had been entranced by the beauty of the Dordogne.

Then her breath had been taken away by the *Château* and the four fountains playing in front of it.

She felt as they walked inside that she was stepping into a fairy-story.

When they had entered the *Salon* it was undoubtedly Prince Charming who came towards them.

The *Duc* was in every respect entirely different from what she had expected.

To begin with, he was much taller than most Frenchmen.

With his broad shoulders and narrow hips, he also looked exceedingly athletic.

As he greeted her Father she thought that he was the most handsome man she had ever seen, certainly very different from what she had imagined he would look like.

It was, she thought, difficult to put into words, but there was an alertness about the *Duc* which made him unmistakably unique.

Marcia held out her hand and dropped a small curtsy.

As she did so, she was aware that the expression in the *Duc*'s eyes was no longer warm and welcoming as it had been to her Father.

Instead, he looked at her with what she could describe only as an expression of dislike.

In a very different tone of voice he said:

"But of course, My Lord, we can accommodate your daughter. My Aunt, the *Comtesse* de Soissons, whom I think you know, will arrange it."

He turned abruptly, as he spoke, towards the *Comtesse*, who was moving towards them.

Even as she greeted the Earl and he introduced Marcia, the *Duc* walked away.

They proceeded towards the Tea Table that was near the fire-place.

As they reached it, Marcia was aware that the *Duc*, talking to the most beautiful woman she could imagine, had his back towards them.

chapter three

THE Duke was furious.

He knew exactly what was afoot the moment he saw Marcia enter the room with her Father.

Because he was so perceptive, he had been aware that there was something "in the air" as far as his Aunt the *Comtesse* was concerned.

He had, however, not really expected that she would actually produce a prospective Bride for him, even though she talked about it incessantly.

She had also, he thought, been discussing it with the other relations.

He had noticed, though it was nothing unusual, that as soon as he entered the room there was a sudden silence.

But that the Earl of Grateswoode should suddenly produce a daughter was something he had not expected.

The *Duc* was well aware that his refusal to marry was a topic that was talked over hour after hour, week after week, year after year.

His relatives tried in every possible way to convince

him that he must do his duty to the Family name and produce an Heir.

There would be no difficulty whatever about it.

Just as when he was young, every great Family in France would be only too eager to ally themselves with the Roux.

And yet the whole idea of it made him shudder.

The ghost of Cecilia stood between him and any prospective Bride.

Now the *Comtesse* had gone a step further and paraded one for him.

Because he had learnt to control himself ever since he was a child, he managed to hide his feelings.

He talked to the *Marquise* in his usual flirtatious manner with every other word having a double meaning.

She was witty and amusing where the subject of Love was concerned.

Yet the *Duc* was already aware that on other subjects she was either palpably ignorant or uninterested.

For the moment, however, because he was so angry, he made himself admire the beauty of her features and the blue lights in her hair.

The provocative invitation in her eyes was very alluring.

That was something to which he was accustomed.

The *Comtesse* was busily introducing the Earl and Marcia to the other guests.

Several more who were staying in the house came in after their arrival.

The *Comtesse* sat at the Tea Table and poured out the tea.

The Earl sat down beside her and said:

"It is very kind of you to remember that Marcia and I enjoyed our Tea, when I know that you do not have it in France."

"It is so delightful to have you here," the *Comtesse* answered, "that I want you both to feel at home."

She lowered her voice so that no-one else could hear her:

"Your daughter is even lovelier than I thought possible. Everyone was talking about her in London, but her beauty is quite breath-taking."

"That is what I think myself," the Earl replied. "But then, I am, of course, a proud Father."

"A very, very proud one, I should imagine," the *Comtesse* answered.

Marcia was talking to two of the *Duc*'s Cousins.

Several men who had just arrived were obviously eager to join in the conversation.

Occasionally she glanced across the room towards the *Duc*.

He was still in deep conversation with the same very attractive woman.

For a moment she thought it was strange that he was apparently ignoring her Father, whom he had been so eager to see.

Then a knowing glance between two of the older relations revealed the truth.

Marcia could not help finding it amusing that the *Duc* was no less antagonistic than she was to the idea of an arranged marriage.

She guessed, too, that he had not been forewarned of her arrival.

That would account for the strange expression in his eyes when he had looked at her.

'I shall have to tell him that I feel exactly the same about the situation,' she thought.

She even had a wild idea of announcing it to the Family, now that they were all gathered together.

She wanted to tell them that she had been brought here against her wish.

If they thought she intended to marry their precious *Duc,* they were very much mistaken!

She could imagine how horrified their expressions would be at her being so out-spoken.

Then she remembered that it would deeply hurt and embarrass her Father.

It was therefore something she could not do.

Because she was hungry, she ate a good Tea, enjoying the delicious *patisseries* that the Chef had provided.

She refused the cucumber sandwiches over which he had taken so much trouble, but the Earl ate two.

When Tea was over the *Comtesse* said:

"I am sure, Lady Marcia, that you would like to see your room."

"That would be delightful," Marcia replied. "At the same time, as you were such a friend of Mama's, I do hope you will call me 'Marcia.' "

The *Comtesse* put her hand on Marcia's arm.

"Of course I shall do that. But as we have not met since you were a very small child, I did not wish you to think I was being too familiar."

They both laughed, and Marcia said:

"I am thrilled to see this entrancing *Château,* and I hope I shall have time to go over it all before we return to England."

"There will be time for you to do that," the *Comtesse* promised. "And to see the horses."

She had risen from the Tea Table.

As if she was aware that her nephew was behaving in a somewhat unfriendly manner, she said to him, raising her voice a little:

"I was just talking to Marcia about your horses,

Armond. I am sure she is as eager to see them as her Father is."

Reluctantly the *Duc* rose to his feet.

"The Earl has come to see my horses," he said. "And of course they are available for anyone else who is interested in them."

He spoke coldly.

As his eyes rested on Marcia she was once again aware that he was looking at her as if he wanted to protest at her intrusion.

Because she wished to provoke him a little, she walked a few steps nearer and said:

"I have heard so much about your *Château,* your horses, and, of course, yourself, *Monsieur,* that I feel now I am here, it cannot be real."

She felt as she spoke that the *Comtesse* was pleased with her and was feeling like a Conjuror.

She had produced a rabbit out of a hat at exactly the right moment.

The *Duc,* however, was not beguiled.

Almost rudely he walked passed Marcia to reach the Earl.

"I have a great deal to talk about to you, My Lord," he said. "I suggest we go somewhere quiet, where we will not be disturbed by the chatter of women—lovely as they may be."

The Earl smiled.

"I feel that they would soon be bored by the subject of our conversation."

"That is what I thought," the *Duc* agreed.

"The exception being," the Earl went on, "my daughter, Marcia, who is as knowledgeable as I am on the breeding of Champions and who is exceedingly interested in seeing your Stud."

The *Duc* did not answer.

He started moving towards the door, and the Earl went with him.

It was quite obvious to Marcia that she was excluded.

She thought it would be a mistake if her Father approached the *Duc* immediately and suggested they should be married.

The *Duc* might resent it.

She went upstairs beside the *Comtesse*.

Then she reassured herself that there was nothing she could do about it and that her Father was a very tactful man and would therefore, in his own words, not be inclined to jump the gun.

The bed-room into which she was shown was magnificent.

The huge canopied bed had been there for generations.

The Aubusson carpet seemed to be a reflection of the colours of the painted ceiling depicting Venus surrounded by Cupids.

"I felt sure you would enjoy this room," the *Comtesse* was saying. "And the pictures by Fragonard make it very romantic."

"It is exquisite," Marcia exclaimed in all sincerity.

At the same time, she felt as if she were walking into a trap.

A beautifully-decorated, softly-padded trap, but nevertheless a trap!

She wondered if she should tell the *Comtesse* frankly and without mincing her words why she was here.

She wanted to say that she had come with her Father as the *Comtesse* had suggested, but she had no intention of marrying the *Duc*.

However hard she and her Father might try to get them to the altar, it was something she would never do.

"It is so delightful to have you here," the *Comtesse* was saying in her soft voice. "You are very like your Mother, whom I loved and thought was the most beautiful person I had ever seen."

"I love to hear you say that," Marcia answered. "And it is a nice change for Papa to come to France. He has been so miserable and unhappy since Mama died that I feel it is good for him to get away from home, where everything reminds him of what he has lost."

"I can understand that," the *Comtesse* said sympathetically, "and your Father is a very remarkable and very clever man."

"You must try and cheer him up," Marcia said. "As he likes being with you and of course seeing the *Duc's* horses, I am sure he will be happy."

She thought as she spoke that this might take the pressure off herself.

She knew the *Comtesse* was listening intently to what she had said.

"I promise you, Dearest Child," the *Comtesse* replied, "that I will do everything in my power to try and make your Father happy and, of course, I want to make you happy too."

Marcia realised that she might go on to say something intimate. Quickly, so as to prevent it, she said:

"I am happy. Happy to be here and to see France for the first time. I only wish I could stay for a time in Paris, having heard so much about the amusements there. I am really quite envious of those who have had the chance to enjoy them."

"I think, my Dear," the *Comtesse* said, "that you are thinking of the amusements that men find in Paris but are not for us women. Except, of course, we have Frederick Worth and all the great *Couturiers* to attract us."

"Have you many gowns made by Worth?" Marcia asked. "Do please let me see them. I have always been told they are the most original that any woman can buy."

She felt she had changed the subject very skilfully.

A moment later the Housekeeper knocked on the door and came in with the maid who was to look after her.

"I did not bring my lady's-maid with me," Marcia explained to the *Comtesse,* "for the simple reason that I thought she would feel out of her depth in not being able to speak a word of French. Papa, however, has brought his Valet, who speaks it well with a Cockney accent."

The *Comtesse* laughed at this.

Marcia, in her perfect Parisian French, talked to the Housekeeper and to the maid.

It was the one thing in the strange education that her Father had planned for her on which her Mother had been insistent.

"I always think it is terrible that we are insular in England," her Mother had said, "so learn the languages of other countries. I am grateful that I started to learn French when I was quite a small child, and Marcia must do the same."

She added, "I think it would also be wise for her to know Spanish and Italian, as those are countries she will enjoy when she travels."

Because with her boy's education Marcia was learning Greek and Latin, she found all languages easy.

She prided herself on being able to read all the books in the Library which her ancestors had collected on their journeys round the world.

When Marcia had taken off the small hat in which she had travelled, the *Comtesse* showed her the *Boudoir.*

It opened out of her bed-room and contained some

beautiful pictures and a ceiling on which the central figure was again that of Venus.

Marcia realised that everything around her was designed to create an impression of Love.

She thought it rather sad that the *Comtesse*'s clearly thought-out plan would fail.

While the stage-setting was right, the two principal characters—the hero and the heroine—were antagonistic to the theme of the Play itself.

The *Comtesse* then showed Marcia some of the other State-Rooms and finally took her into the *Duc*'s suite, which was naturally the most important in the whole *Château*.

It occupied the whole end of the building with windows looking East, West, and South.

He had therefore a bird's-eye view of the valley sweeping below him down to the Vineyards.

Through the centre of it flowed a silver river, while the cliffs rose on the far side to complete the picture.

The great gorges were magnificent, but at the same time awe-inspiring.

Marcia felt she could understand the *Duc*'s satisfaction in being the owner of something so fantastic.

There were, in fact, she decided, no words with which to describe what she could see.

She could only stand at the window, thinking the panoramic view, if nothing else, was something she would never forget.

The *Duc*'s rooms themselves were almost as impressive as his Estate.

The huge bed, reaching to the ceiling, was like the throne of the Pope hung with crimson velvet curtains, the Coat of Arms of the de Roux Family embroidered at the head.

On the low posts at the foot of the bed there were two exquisitely carved figures of kneeling angels.

"No wonder he thinks himself so important," Marcia murmured.

She did not miss what was almost a note of awe in the *Comtesse*'s voice as she explained how everything had been collected down the ages.

She implied they were almost sanctified by being in the possession of the *Duc* de Roux.

As they came out of the *Duc*'s suite into the corridor, Marcia was aware that there was a young man walking towards them.

He appeared rather good-looking, and as he approached, the *Comtesse* exclaimed:

"Sardos, where have you been? We missed you at Tea."

"I have been riding," he said briefly. "Alone, because I wanted to think."

"You missed the arrival of the Earl of Grateswoode," the *Comtesse* said. "So let me present you to his daughter."

She turned to Marcia.

"This is our host's nephew, Sardos de Thiviers."

Marcia put out her hand, and Sardos took it in his.

As he did so, she had the unmistakable feeling that there was something sinister about the young man.

She wondered why she should feel like that and told herself she must be mistaken.

"I was told by my friends who have seen you in London how beautiful you are," Sardos said in his most honeyed voice, "but they were obviously not able to find words to describe you adequately."

It was very prettily said.

Yet even as he spoke, Marcia felt there was something hostile behind his words.

The expression in his eyes certainly denied the smile on his lips.

"Thank you," she replied. "But I have always been warned not to believe compliments which are paid by the French far too easily and too fluently."

For a moment Sardos was surprised at her reply, and then he said:

"And I have always been told that English women do not know how to receive a compliment. But of course you will have had so many that you have merely become bored with them."

The *Comtesse* was listening with amusement.

Then it struck her that the last thing she wanted at this moment was Sardos interfering with her scheme to bring the *Duc* and Marcia together.

"I do not know why you are in this corridor, Sardos," she said almost sharply. "I, in fact, am taking Lady Marcia to her *Boudoir*."

"I was looking for you," Sardos replied. "I thought if you were not busy, I should like to have a talk with you."

The *Comtesse* looked at him sharply.

"Later," she said. "There are so many guests in the house, you will understand that I have not much time to myself."

"I still want to talk to you," Sardos insisted.

"We will see about it," she replied lightly.

She slipped her arm through Marcia's and drew her towards the door of her *Boudoir*.

The *Comtesse* was aware as she did so that Sardos gave her a sharp glance.

As she opened the door she was sure he was aware of the reason Marcia had been given those particular rooms.

As she deliberately shut him outside, she thought that it was very unfortunate that he had turned up at the *Château*.

She wanted there to be nothing to distract the *Duc* from becoming friendly, and a great deal more than that, with the Earl's daughter.

"Who is that young man?" Marcia asked when they were in the *Boudoir* and the door was shut.

"He is a very tiresome creature," the *Comtesse* said sharply. "He is the *Duc*'s nephew and permanently in debt."

Marcia looked surprised, and she explained:

"He enjoys the 'amusements' in Paris that you were just talking about, but unfortunately they are very expensive.

"He neglects his Mother and his Estate, which is in Normandy."

She sighed before she went on:

"His Uncle has been very generous to him, but he is not in the least grateful, and I suspect that the reason he is here now is to demand more money to pay off his debts."

'That is just what I might have expected,' Marcia thought.

It explained the strange feeling she had had when she shook hands with Sardos de Thiviers.

"Now, what I am sure you would like is to have a rest before Dinner," the *Comtesse* was saying. "Personally I always feel not only exhausted after a journey but somewhat dirty until I can have a bath."

She passed from the *Boudoir* into the bed-room, where the maid had nearly finished unpacking.

"*Mademoiselle* would like a bath before Dinner," she said to her. "Until then she will rest."

The *Comtesse* then said to Marcia:

"You must look your loveliest, my dear, to-night, as I am sure you will, and to-morrow we will arrange a special party with all the most charming people in the neighbourhood to meet you."

"Thank you," Marcia said. "But you know that what I really want to meet are the *Duc*'s horses."

"You shall do that," the *Comtesse* answered, "but we can hardly ask them into the Banqueting-Hall for Dinner!"

She glanced round the room as if to make sure that everything was in place. Marcia thought that the whole place vibrated with the beauty and the splendour of Love.

She undressed and lay down in the great bed.

As she did so, she told herself she would have to fight valiantly against enemies which were soft and gentle rather than hard and forceful.

"I am beginning to think," she said to herself, "that the only person on my side will be the *Duc*."

Downstairs the *Duc* and the Earl had talked exclusively about their horses and to the satisfaction of them both.

The *Duc* imparted all the new ideas he had absorbed in Hungary.

The Earl responded with some experiments he had made in his stables at Newmarket, which had proved extremely successful.

Finally it was with reluctance that they realised that time was getting on and they must go upstairs to change for Dinner.

"It is delightful to have you here," the *Duc* said as they rose to their feet.

"I have been hoping for a long time to be your guest," the Earl said. "But there have always been some reasons to prevent my coming to France."

"But now you are here," the *Duc* answered, "we must certainly make the most of it."

They walked up the stairs together.

There was a footman waiting to show the Earl where he was sleeping.

It was another State-Room which was very much more masculine than the one occupied by Marcia.

But it contained every comfort, and the Earl's Valet was busy arranging a bath for him.

The servants had carried huge brass cans of hot and cold water up the stairs with which to fill it.

The *Duc* left the Earl and went to his own Suite.

As he went down the passage he saw a maid coming out of the room that had been his Mother's.

He guessed at once that that was where his uninvited guest, the Earl's daughter, was sleeping.

Instantly his anger rose again.

He realised that the *Comtesse* had deliberately put Lady Marcia there because it was the room she would occupy if she became his wife.

He went into his own Suite and slammed the door.

He told himself that it was intolerable that he could not be left alone.

His Aunt, of whom, in fact, he was very fond, had no right to be intriguing in such a blatant way with the Earl to try to push him into marrying.

"Why cannot I be left alone?" he asked himself, and went to the window to look out.

It was something that had never ceased to thrill him.

He looked down the valley with its abundance of vines, and thought that no woman could give him the same pleasure as producing a good harvest.

No woman could look so lovely as the silver streak

of the river curving between trees that had a fairy-like appearance about them.

'It is mine, mine,' he thought. 'I will not share it with anyone.'

His Valet came into the room to help him undress.

The *Duc* did not speak, and the man, who knew all his moods, realised that something had upset him.

He thought it must be *Monsieur* Sardos, as there was inevitably trouble whenever he appeared.

'A tiresome young man if ever there was one,' he thought to himself. 'I wouldn't trust him farther than I could throw a pebble.'

He was too discreet, however, to express such sentiments aloud.

He merely helped the *Duc,* after he had bathed, into his evening-clothes.

If he looked impressive in what he wore in the daytime, the *Duc* was in the evening completely outstanding.

It would have been impossible to ignore him even if there had been a thousand other men in the same room.

An observer might have said the same of Marcia.

She came from her bed-room wearing one of the attractive gowns she had bought in London at the beginning of the Season.

She had not made the mistake that so many girls did of being over-resplendent or too elaborate.

Although her relatives were only too willing to advise her, she had always chosen what she liked for herself.

It was always simplicity enhanced by a touch of genius which made it a perfect frame for her beauty.

She did not think of it like that.

But those who designed the clothes she ordered realised that she knew better than what the fashion decreed.

In consequence, they produced something original,

something which in itself might have been a picture from the brush of a famous artist or a poem from the pen of an inspired poet.

Tonight, and Marcia was thinking of the *Château* and not the *Duc,* she wore a gown that was a very soft shade of blue.

It toned with the blue which Boucher had used in his pictures and Fragonard in his.

She wore no jewellery except a string of pearls which had belonged to her Mother.

She swept downstairs, her hair shining in the rays coming from the setting sun.

She might have been a young goddess moving down from the peaks into the valley of the mortals.

When she entered the *Salon d'Or,* all eyes turned towards her.

She was aware that there was admiration in all of them with one exception.

The *Duc* was standing in his habitual position with his back to the fire-place.

It seemed to Marcia as she moved towards him that they were ready to duel with each other with invisible swords and were both "on guard."

Then, just before she reached him, the *Duc* once again turned as if someone had spoken to him.

Marcia found herself facing not him but Sardos.

"We meet again, Lady Marcia," he said. "May I tell you that every picture in the *Château* pales before you?"

Again he was complimenting her.

Marcia, however, had a feeling that a sudden thought had occurred to him when she was approaching the *Duc,* and that he was disconcerted by it.

She did not know why she should think such a thing, but it was undoubtedly in her mind.

Then as her Father joined her, she slipped her arm through his.

"I know you have had a lovely time, Papa, talking about horses, but I missed you."

"And I missed you, my Dearest," he said. "To-morrow we will go together to inspect them and, of course, to see if we can find something to criticise, because we cannot allow them to be as good as those we own."

They both laughed.

Marcia, however, was aware that her Father was looking at the *Duc* as if he thought he should have been at her side.

He was, however, as she expected, talking to the beautiful *Marquise*.

She was obviously determined to out-gown every other woman in the room.

She was wearing a dress of vivid pink which accentuated the whiteness of her skin and the darkness of her hair.

As she stood beside the *Duc*, Marcia thought that they were an outstandingly handsome couple.

She wondered, if he had to marry anyone, why he did not marry someone as alluring as the *Marquise*.

It was a question that made her curious, and she could not help asking when she sat down at Dinner if the *Marquise* was married.

She was speaking to Sardos because, to her surprise, she found she was sitting next to him.

It was correct for the *Marquise* to be on the *Duc*'s right, Marcia thought.

But as a foreigner and because of her Title, she felt she should have been on his left.

She thought it was a quite deliberate decision on his part.

He had put her between Sardos and another younger man who was unmarried.

'I suppose,' she thought with a smile, 'he is hoping I shall be snatched away at the precise moment when he should be asking for my hand in Marriage.'

Once again she could not help feeling how amusing it was that she and the *Duc* were allies in fighting desperately against everyone else.

"Of course she is married," Sardos answered in response to Marcia's question. "The *Marquis* is, however, at the moment in Rome on a very important mission on behalf of the Government."

Marcia realised that that was the end of her idea of marrying the *Duc* to the *Marquise*.

Despite the fact that she behaved with every discretion, the *Marquise* could not control her eyes.

The way she looked at the *Duc*, Marcia thought, made it very obvious even to the most obtuse observer where her interests lay.

He was far more controlled.

Many thought it was difficult to guess how deep his feeling was for the lovely woman on his right.

But it did just strike her that they might be lovers.

Despite her two Seasons in London, Marcia was very innocent.

Unlike many of her contemporaries, she never talked about love and was not interested in gossip.

It was a waste of time, she thought, to speculate on any relationship between a man and a woman unless it was published in the *Gazette*.

She had, therefore, not listened to the whispers of those around her.

Nor did she heed the wailing of the girls when some man they fancied was spirited away from them by some sophisticated married woman.

She was thinking about the *Duc* when Sardos asked sharply:

"Why are you here? Someone told me you were not expected."

"I am afraid I am a Gate-crasher," Marcia answered. "The *Duc* had invited my Father to come and see his horses, and as he particularly wanted me to travel with him, I came at the last moment."

She saw, as she spoke, that Sardos was frowning. "You have not met my Uncle before?" he asked.

She shook her head.

"But of course I have heard about him and his horses."

"I suppose you know," Sardos said, "that my relations are all of them trying to persuade him to marry again. Do you think of yourself in the role of his Bride?"

He spoke so rudely that Marcia looked at him in surprise.

Then she answered quietly:

"I can assure you that I have no intention of marrying the *Duc* or, for that matter, anyone else."

She thought that the expression in Sardos's eyes cleared a little.

At the same time, she knew he was still suspicious, as he looked down the table at the *Duc* and then back at her.

"I have a feeling," he said after a moment, "that the *Comtesse* is at the bottom of this."

"The bottom of what?" Marcia asked lightly. "If you are trying to make a drama out of my appearance, all I can tell you is I intend to travel back to England with my Father when he is ready to go as free and unfettered as I am at the moment."

"But of course," Sardos said as if he were reasoning it

out for himself, "you would be a very suitable Bride for Uncle Armond."

"I heard, though I may have been misinformed," Marcia replied, "that he has no wish to marry anyone."

"That is what he has said," Sardos answered. "At the same time, he will be forced eventually to produce an Heir, and that, of course, means less money will be available for relations like myself."

Marcia remembered what had been said about him, but she answered somewhat mockingly:

"No-one round this table looks as though they were poverty-stricken."

"Looks are deceptive," Sardos snapped. "If you want the truth, I am on the point of being taken to Prison for Debts I cannot meet."

"I cannot believe the *Duc* would allow that to happen." Marcia smiled.

"That is what I hope," Sardos said. "But he is mean and extremely cheese-paring where I am concerned."

He almost spat out his words.

Marcia was wondering what to say, when the gentleman on her other side complained:

"You are neglecting me, Lady Marcia."

She turned to smile at him.

"Then that is something I must remedy at once. Suppose you tell me what is your particular interest."

"I have two," the man replied. "One is the excellent wines which come from my Host's Vineyards in the valley. The second is my horses, which I believe are the reason that you have come here with your Father."

"You are quite right," Marcia replied. "I am looking forward more than I can possibly say to seeing them tomorrow."

It was exciting to talk about horses, and for the moment Marcia forgot Sardos.

Then, when Dinner was coming to an end, he said to her in a low voice:

"If you mean what you say, and have no wish to be incarcerated here for the rest of your life, you must be careful. My relatives are all determined to fetter you to my Uncle."

"I think you are talking nonsense," Marcia answered.

At the same time, there was a note in Sardos's voice that made her shiver.

She thought, as she had the first moment she met him, that there was something not only sinister about him but almost evil.

She was glad when everyone had left the Dining-Room.

As was the custom in France, the men did not stay behind as in England.

Everyone went into the *Salon,* and there were card-tables arranged for those who wished to play.

An accomplished pianist was sitting at the piano, playing soft music which was just a background for the conversation.

Nothing, Marcia thought, could be more delightful.

Yet as she watched the *Comtesse* look round she had the feeling that it was all arranged for one purpose and one purpose only.

That was to bind her and the *Duc* together as man and wife.

chapter four

HAVING arranged for everybody to be seated at the card-tables, the *Comtesse* realised that the Earl was sitting alone at the far end of the *Salon*.

She walked towards him, saying as she reached him:

"Do not get up. I presume you do not wish to play cards."

"I would much rather talk to you," the Earl replied.

"That is what I have been hoping for," the *Comtesse* answered.

They sat down on the sofa, and she said in her soft voice:

"It was so kind of you to come. I have been so desperately worried and could not think to whom I could turn. Then I remembered you."

"I am flattered," the Earl answered. "But I do not like you to be upset or worried. You have always seemed to me to be such a serene person."

"That is what I try to be," the *Comtesse* replied, "but things are difficult and I am very, very worried about Armond."

"About his not marrying?" the Earl asked.

"That is the beginning of it," the *Comtesse* said, "and it is why I asked you to bring your exquisite daughter here with you."

The Earl was about to say that Marcia too was being difficult about being married.

Then he thought it would be a mistake.

He would listen first to what the *Comtesse* had to say.

She was looking so worried that he was quite certain that it was somewhat worse than he had thought.

In her late forties, the *Comtesse* was still a beautiful woman.

She was very young when she married, and her husband had been much older than herself.

The Earl had often thought they were ill-matched because of the difference in age.

When the *Comtesse* became a widow he had hoped that she would marry again.

But from what he had learnt from the letters that passed between them, she was devoting herself to her nephew, the *Duc*.

As he had no wife, she acted as his Hostess.

Now, as he saw the anxiety in her eyes, he put his hand over hers.

"You know," he said, "that I will help you in any way I can, and because we are such old friends you must allow me to call you Yvonne, as my wife did."

"That is what I would like," the *Comtesse* replied, "and thank you, Lionel, for being a tower of strength."

"It is what I hope to be," the Earl said as he smiled, "but you have not yet told me what is amiss."

The *Comtesse* glanced towards the card-players as if to make sure they could not be overheard.

Then she said:

"I think you may have guessed that it is Sardos who is at the bottom of the trouble."

"I am not surprised," the Earl replied. "He is a very tiresome young man and always has been!"

"Far more than tiresome!" the *Comtesse* said. "He is spending so much money that not only Armond, but all our relatives, are in a frantic state because, believe it or not, if he goes on like this, he will impoverish the Estate."

The Earl looked at her in surprise.

"I can hardly imagine that is possible," he remarked, "considering that the *Duc* is known to be one of the richest men in France."

"He has a great Estate and a wonderful *Château* with, as you know, many exquisite treasures in it," the *Comtesse* replied. "But with regard to money—he spreads it fairly and generously amongst us all."

She sighed before she went on:

"Sardos, however, has had much more than his share and his Mother's combined."

"That is disgraceful!" the Earl exclaimed. "I hope your nephew has remonstrated with him very forcefully."

"The last time he was here," the *Comtesse* said, "Armond told him that if he came begging again, he would give him nothing. Sardos must starve rather than deprive the rest of the Family of what is our right."

"And I suppose you are telling me that once again he is in debt," the Earl said slowly.

"It is much worse than that," the *Comtesse* said.

"How?" the Earl enquired.

"I have friends in Paris," the *Comtesse* began, "who regularly send me information as to what Sardos is doing."

She looked at the Earl a little pleadingly as she added:

"I am not really spying on him just for the sake of it, but to save Armond from any further embarrassment."

"I understand—of course I understand!" the Earl murmured.

"Some weeks ago," the *Comtesse* continued, "I was told that Sardos was in desperate trouble. He owes thousands and thousands of *francs* and his Creditors are becoming extremely unpleasant about it."

The Earl thought it was what he might have suspected.

He too had heard of Sardos's extravagance on women who could spend a man's whole fortune in two or three days and nights.

"That was bad news," the *Comtesse* continued, "but there is worse . . ."

"In what way?" the Earl enquired.

"I was told confidentially that Sardos was assuring his Creditors that his Uncle would not live for very long. On his death, as there was no direct Heir, the money and the Estate would belong to his Mother."

The Earl stared at the *Comtesse* in astonishment.

"Is that true?" he asked.

"It is something I had not thought about," the *Comtesse* admitted. "In fact, I have been so certain that sooner or later Armond would marry again that I had never asked what would happen if he died. After all, he is not yet thirty."

"I know that," the Earl said. "But, surely, there is some Heir Presumptive if he does not have a son himself."

"Actually the title would end with Armond," the *Comtesse* replied, "which is why we have been so worried."

She paused for a moment before she continued:

"My brother, Armond's Father, longed to have a large Family. As is usual, he was married when he was young to a charming girl whom we all liked."

The Earl nodded his head, and the *Comtesse* went on:

"She produced a daughter, then learnt from the Doctors that it would be impossible for her to have another child."

"I had no idea of this," the Earl exclaimed. "In fact, I always thought that the *Duc* was the son of the first marriage."

The *Comtesse* shook her head.

"No, Eleonore died of a sudden fever four years after they were married."

The Earl was listening intently as she continued:

"To our delight, my brother married again, and while he had been happy with his first wife, we all adored Dorothée, who was the sweetest person and as lovely in her own way as your wife."

"And what happened?" the Earl asked.

The *Comtesse* sighed again.

"She produced Armond," she answered, "a year after the marriage, and you can imagine how thrilled my brother was. Armond was not only the direct Heir, but also the most adored child you could imagine. From the moment he was born he seemed to be everything that a Father and Mother could want. Naturally Dorothée wanted other children so that he would have companions."

"And that was not possible?"

"It was a cruel blow and it is difficult to understand why God was not more merciful," the *Comtesse* replied. "But a year after Armond was born, Dorothée had a fall out riding and her horse rolled on her."

The Earl made an exclamation of horror, but he did not interrupt.

"My brother sent for every Specialist in the whole

country, but there was nothing they could do. For a long time she was in great pain, but that passed and eventually it would have been difficult for any outsider to guess there was anything wrong. The real misery of it was that she could not have another child."

"It is the saddest story I have ever heard," the Earl exclaimed, "and had no idea that anything like that had happened."

"It was never talked about in the Family because it upset my brother so much. And in fact, because Armond was delightful and so skilled at everything he undertook, we never missed the younger brothers and sisters he should have had."

"I can understand that."

The Earl was thinking of the *Duc's* athletic prowess and how brilliant he was with horses.

"In fact, everything seemed perfect," the *Comtesse* said, "until there was the catastrophe of Armond's Marriage which was really my brother's fault."

"Why do you say that?" the Earl asked.

"Because he was in such a hurry for Armond to have an Heir, he insisted on his marrying when he was really too young. Having chosen his wife, my brother did not, we realised later, make enough enquiries about the girl herself."

The *Comtesse* gave a deep sigh that seemed to come from the depths of her body.

"How could we have imagined—how could we have guessed—that she was mad? Of course her parents, the *Marquis* and *Marquise* knew about it, but they were desperately eager for her to become *la Duchesse* de Roux."

"It was a wicked act on their part, and I hope they suffered when the Truth came out," the Earl remarked.

"They suffered," the *Comtesse* agreed, "but it was

Armond who was left with a hatred of Marriage and a determination to do anything rather than go through the horror of it again."

"A natural reaction," the Earl murmured sympathetically.

"But now there is this problem with Sardos."

"You do not really believe he would murder his Uncle to get the money he so badly needs?" the Earl asked.

"I can hardly bear to think of it," the *Comtesse* confessed. "But because he has always been an unpleasant, if not evil, young man, I feel he would stick at nothing to get money and more money, having spent a fortune already."

"What does his Mother think of all this?" the Earl asked.

"She has been in poor health for a long time," the *Comtesse* answered, "and never leaves her home in Normandy—in fact, the Doctors say she is not well enough to travel."

She gave a little sob before she went on:

"What we do know is that the money Armond gives her is all snatched away by Sardos. He goes home only when there is a chance of his being able to take money from his Mother which Armond has sent her."

"It is utterly disgraceful!" the Earl exclaimed. "Something should be done about that young man!"

"I agree with you," the *Comtesse* said. "The difficulty is—what can we do? If anything should happen to Armond, the money and Estate goes to his half-sister."

The Earl made an exclamation, and the *Comtesse* explained:

"My brother made a Will soon after Armond was born in which he said, of course, that everything went, as is usual in France, to the next Heir to the Dukedom. In the event, however, of there being no Heir, then the money should be divided between his daughter by his first marriage and the children who would, of course, in that case all be daughters that Armond produced."

The Earl thought this over.

Then he said:

"I see. That means that in the present circumstances, if the *Duc* dies unmarried and leaving no Heir, then his half-sister inherits everything."

"Everything!" the *Comtesse* affirmed. "And that is what Sardos has told his Creditors."

The Earl once again put his hand over hers.

"I understand how much this is frightening you," he said, "but I cannot believe that in this day and age your nephew Sardos would risk going to the guillotine. If he murdered his Uncle, that is exactly what would happen."

"Only if he were found out," the *Comtesse* said in a low voice.

"He may be a spend-thrift and, as you say, cruel to his Mother. But I cannot believe that any man of his age would risk being arrested for murder!" the Earl objected.

He saw the *Comtesse* shiver and went on:

"Should the *Duc* die in circumstances that could arouse any suspicion, that suspicion would immediately rest on anyone who was likely to benefit from his death."

"I appreciate what you are saying," the *Comtesse* replied. "At the same time, I am frightened, very frightened! I have never liked Sardos. I have always been horrified at the way he treats his Mother."

She looked at the Earl before she said:

"I am well aware that he will swear on everything Holy that he will not get into debt again. But he makes no effort to keep his vow."

"I agree with you that the whole situation is appalling," the Earl answered. "I am only wondering what I can do about it."

"You have done exactly what I asked you to do," the *Comtesse* replied. "You have brought your daughter here. Surely Armond will see how lovely she is and how very suitable a marriage would be between your Family and ours?"

The Earl hesitated.

Then he said:

"I must be frank with you, Yvonne, and I am afraid it will upset you, but Marcia is determined not to marry the *Duc,* or any other man for that matter!"

The *Comtesse* stared at him.

"Determined not to be married?" she said slowly.

"Marcia has turned down every eligible bachelor in London," the Earl replied, "including, just before we came here, the Duke of Buckstead."

"And you do not think she will be attracted to Armond?"

"I only hope that she will change her mind," the Earl said slowly, "but she told me categorically that nothing would induce her to marry the *Duc,* and she would not allow me to choose a husband for her even though she is aware that by the Laws of England I can force her to marry any man I wish to have as a son-in-law."

The *Comtesse* gave a little cry.

"Oh, Lionel, then all my plans are hopeless! I was praying as I have prayed fervently that these two young people would fall in love with each other, and if there was an Heir, Sardos would gain nothing by murdering Armond."

The Earl wondered what he could say to comfort her.

Finally, after a moment, he said:

"I hope, Yvonne, that things are not really as bad as you suspect. Would you like me to speak to Sardos and try to make him see sense?"

"He will pay no attention to you," the *Comtesse* replied. "Or, rather, he would agree to do anything you asked of him, especially if you gave him some money. Then, as soon as you had left, he would go on exactly as he has before. I have lost count of all the times this has happened with Armond."

"It does seem very difficult," the Earl said in a low voice. "At the same time, I cannot believe that Sardos will risk his neck by attempting to murder the *Duc*."

"If he can find a way of doing it without anybody realising it is he, he will do it!" the *Comtesse* asserted.

She spoke so positively that the Earl was startled.

Then he thought perhaps she was being a little hysterical, and in a conciliatory tone he said:

"I have a feeling that things are not as bad as you anticipate, and I am hoping perhaps their interest in horses will bring the *Duc* and Marcia together. You know, nothing would make me happier than for my Family to be allied with yours."

"It is something I should welcome with open arms," the *Comtesse* said. "You and Elizabeth were always the perfect couple and your home was such a happy one. I have never forgotten its atmosphere of peace and, of course, Love."

The Earl was very moved.

"Thank you, Yvonne," he said. "I think you understand how lonely I have been without my wife, and what a joy it has been to have Marcia with me, growing up so beautiful with a character which matches her looks."

"She is just what I want for Armond's wife," the

Comtesse sighed. "Oh, Lionel, do you think God will ever hear my prayers?"

"I know that no-one could pray more sincerely than you do," the Earl answered, "and we must, my Dear, just hope that things will come right."

* — * — *

Marcia enjoyed her game of cards with the two men and the very charming woman who made up the table.

She was, however, glad when the *Comtesse* announced that as some of their guests had been travelling, they should all go to bed early.

"I am rather tired, Papa," Marcia said to the Earl.

"So am I, my Dearest," the Earl answered.

They walked together into the Hall.

As they reached the stairs they were aware that the *Duc*, with the *Marquise* at his side, were just behind them.

"Good-night, My Lord," the *Duc* said to the Earl. "To-morrow we will have a parade of all my horses for you to see."

"I am looking forward to it!" the Earl replied.

Then, speaking not only to the Earl but to the other members of the house-party who stood round him, the *Duc* went on. "Of course, anyone who wishes to ride early in the morning may do so. We will all assemble later in the paddocks, where I have my race-course at eleven o'clock."

There was a murmur of pleasure when he said this.

As Marcia and the Earl proceeded up the stairs, she said to her Father in a low voice:

"Does that mean we will be able to ride?"

"Of course it does! You may ride any time you like here, but you must be certain to get yourself a really good horse. We will see the parade of the *Duc*'s stables, and after that there will be some flat races in which everybody takes part, and other races with a number of high hedges to be jumped."

Marcia gave a cry of excitement.

"That is what I shall enjoy, Papa, and I hope I do you credit."

"I shall be very angry if you do not!" the Earl teased.

As she reached her bed-room she kissed her Father affectionately.

"Good-night, Papa. It is very exciting being here in the most beautiful *Château* I have ever imagined."

"I thought you would enjoy it," the Earl replied. "I have not been here for many years, but the *Duc* has made it even more beautiful than I remember on my last visit to his Father."

He walked away to his own room and Marcia went into hers.

She was, in fact, very tired, and slept peacefully in the big, comfortable bed.

When she woke, the sun was shining through the sides of the curtains.

She sat up in bed, looked at the clock, and realised it was still very early.

She looked out through the window, and the panoramic view over the valley was breath-taking.

She felt it was impossible to remain in bed, even though she had asked the maid to call her at seven o'clock.

Her Father had said that anybody could ride who wanted to, and there seemed no reason for her to hesitate.

She dressed herself quickly, as she often did at home.

Because it was hot, she put on a riding-skirt that was made of a thin piqué material which had just become fashionable.

It was unnecessary to wear the jacket that went with it.

She omitted a hat because at home she always rode bare-headed.

It was just before six o'clock as she ran down the stairs.

The house-maids in their mob-caps were already cleaning the Hall.

It was obvious as they bobbed a curtsy that they were surprised to see one of the guests so early.

Marcia was sure that nobody else in the party was up at such an early hour.

She had already guessed in which direction the stables lay.

When she reached them, she found that the young grooms had just begun to clean out the stalls.

They were also carrying water and food to the horses.

As she had expected, the stables were magnificent— almost, she thought, as fine as the *Château* itself.

She could not resist moving from one stall to another.

She thought that the occupant of each one was finer than the last.

A groom, who seemed superior to the others, asked her which horse she wished to ride.

"I would love to ride this one!" she replied.

"That is *Aquilin, M'mselle,*" the groom replied, "and one of *Monsieur le Duc*'s favourites."

"I am sure he will not mind if I take him for a short ride," Marcia answered.

The groom was too well-trained to argue.

He merely saddled *Aquilin* and took the horse outside to the mounting-block.

As Marcia seated herself in the saddle, she thought her Father would be hard-pressed to find his equal.

It was not difficult to find her way onto the open ground which sloped down towards the valley.

She soon found a smooth stretch on which she could gallop.

She took *Aquilin* at a speed which made her hair fall into soft curls round her forehead.

Only when she felt that both she and her horse were breathless did she draw *Aquilin* in and move more slowly.

Now she was looking at the great cliffs rising up on one side of her.

Below she could see the Vineyards and the river which ran through them.

"It is lovely, lovely!" she said aloud. "The most beautiful place I could ever imagine!"

She went some way farther before reluctantly turning back towards the *Château*.

Her Father would be coming downstairs for breakfast and, if he intended to ride immediately after it, he would be disappointed if she was not there.

She was trotting *Aquilin* at a slow pace when she became aware that in the distance a rider was coming toward her.

As he drew nearer, it was somehow not surprising to realise it was the *Duc*.

For the first time, Marcia began to wonder if she had not committed a *faux pas*.

Was it wrong to have asked for a horse which the groom had said was one of the *Duc*'s favourites?

There was nothing she could do, however, but ride towards him.

She had to admit, as she watched him, that he rode better than any man she had ever seen.

He was mounted on a huge black stallion.

It was impossible not to appreciate the picture he made on such a magnificent horse.

The cliffs were on one side of him, the trees behind, and far in the distance the white walls of the *Château*.

The *Duc* came closer still.

As he reached Marcia, he swept off his hat.

"Good-morning, Lady Marcia," he said. "I was surprised to find you had stolen my favourite mount!"

"I was afraid you might say that," Marcia replied. "Please forgive me, *Monsieur,* but I just could not resist *Aquilin,* and even if you are angry with me, it is worth it because I have so much enjoyed riding him."

Just for a moment the hard expression in the *Duc*'s eyes softened, as if he was amused by her reply.

Then he asked:

"You are quite certain he is not too much for you?"

"You are insulting me and insulting Papa even more," Marcia answered. "I have ridden since I was in the cradle, and Papa would be furious if he thought anything you could breed would unseat me!"

The *Duc* laughed as if he could not help it.

Then he said:

"As I have no wish to insult your Father, whom I admire tremendously, I can only say you ride as his daughter should."

"Thank you," Marcia said. "I was just going back to the *Château,* as I thought Papa might want to ride after breakfast and wish me to accompany him."

"You do not think you will be too tired after your long ride this morning?" the *Duc* enquired.

Marcia was just about to make a sharp retort, when she realised he was teasing her.

"I will answer that question at the end of the day," she said. "I am looking forward to racing you, *Monsieur,* or shall we make it a Steeple-Chase?"

"Perhaps we might manage both," the *Duc* replied.

"That is a promise," Marcia answered, "and I shall keep you to it!"

The horses were walking side by side.

Marcia suddenly realised this was her opportunity, when nobody could interrupt them, to speak frankly to the *Duc*.

For a moment she hesitated, feeling it was embarrassing.

Then she told herself that the sooner everything was put into its right perspective, the better.

"I had not expected to meet you this morning, *Monsieur*," she began, "but now you are here I have something to say to you, and I am glad of the opportunity."

The *Duc* raised his eye-brows before he replied:

"I am listening, Lady Marcia."

"I think I must tell you," Marcia continued, "that in fact your Aunt the *Comtesse* asked Papa to bring me with him to stay at the *Château,* and I expect you can guess why she did so."

Without even looking at the *Duc* she was aware that he had stiffened.

There was an angry expression in his eyes, and his lips had set in a hard line.

For a moment he contemplated telling Lady Marcia to mind her own business.

Then he thought it would be a mistake to be rude and easier to pretend to be mystified.

"I am afraid, Lady Marcia," he replied, "that I have no idea what you are implying."

"Then I will be frank, *Monsieur*," Marcia answered, "and tell you that your Aunt intimated to Papa that I would make a suitable Bride for you."

The *Duc* drew in his breath.

This was plain speaking such as he had not expected, and he was not at all certain how to answer it.

"What I wanted to tell you," Marcia went on before he could speak, "is that I personally have no wish to marry you and no intention of doing so."

If she had thrown a bomb at him, the *Duc* could not have been more surprised.

He was used to being pleaded with to marry.

He had therefore assumed that any young woman in France or any other country would agree with alacrity to become his wife.

He had been certain without anybody saying so that this was the reason Lady Marcia had been brought to the *Château*.

He thought it was going to be very difficult to inform the Earl, if he raised the question, that he did not wish to marry his daughter.

What he had never anticipated for one moment was that the Earl's daughter would have no wish to become his wife.

Last night, when he had gone to the *Marquise*'s room and made love to her, he had told himself that all he wanted of life was amusement and gratification.

This meant making love to any beautiful woman who would not try to fetter him to her by the Marriage Service.

He had been perturbed by Marcia's sudden appearance, and he had soon guessed that it had been planned to bring them together, and why.

Because of this, he had not enjoyed himself with the *Marquise* as much as he had expected.

She had been very alluring, very passionate, and insatiable in her demands.

It was what he had experienced before, but somehow, although he could not explain it to himself, there was something missing.

He had gone back to his own room sooner than she had expected.

She had reproached him for doing so.

"How can you leave me, dearest Armond," she whispered, "when we are so fortunate to be here together with Eugène away in Rome and no one to interrupt our happiness?"

"Forgive me if I disappoint you," the *Duc* replied, "but I have a great deal to arrange to-morrow, and I have waited a long time to have the Earl of Grateswoode as my guest."

"I also am . . . your guest," the *Marquise* said softly.

"Do you think I could forget that?" the *Duc* answered. "To-morrow night I will tell you again how beautiful you are."

It was not exactly what the *Marquise* wanted, but she had to be content.

She had already learnt that whatever she said and however much she protested, the *Duc* would always do what he wanted.

He left her and went to his bed-room.

But when he got into bed, he did not sleep as he expected to do immediately.

Instead, he lay thinking of how infuriating it was that his Aunt should have arranged with the Earl to bring his daughter with him.

She would spoil what he had thought would be their joint enjoyment of his horses.

"Curse the girl!" he swore to himself. "I would not marry her if she were Aphrodite herself, but I have no wish to tell her Father so."

Yet now, when he had least expected it, the girl he had cursed was telling him before he could speak that she had no wish to be his wife.

Because he was so surprised, he asked the first question that came into his head.

"Why do you have no wish to marry me?" he enquired.

"I should have thought the answer was quite obvious," Marcia replied. "I do not love you, and I have no intention of marrying anyone I do not love."

The *Duc* stared at her.

"But surely," he said, "you will accept someone of whom your Father approves?"

Marcia shook her head.

"I have already told Papa firmly that I will not marry anyone until I am in love. He is determined, however, that I shall marry you, and I can only ask you to make it quite clear that you have no wish to marry me."

The *Duc* was even more astonished than he was already.

He knew that any girl in the length and breadth of France would jump at the opportunity of marrying him.

Her Father and Mother would be even more eager than she was.

It had never struck him for one moment that anyone on whom he even smiled would refuse him their favours.

Yet this young girl, who he admitted reluctantly was exceedingly beautiful, did not wish to be the *Duchesse* de Roux.

It astonished him, to say the least of it.

Aloud he remarked:

"Of course I respect your feelings, Lady Marcia, but I find them somewhat uncomplimentary."

Marcia laughed.

"On the contrary," she said, "you were angry when I arrived, and I was sure then that you had not been told that Papa was bringing me."

She looked at him with her eyes twinkling as she continued:

"You have made it very clear since then that you have no wish for my company, and I have only been waiting for an opportunity to tell you that I share your feelings."

She paused to say almost pleadingly:

"I beg you to plan with me how to save ourselves from being dragged forcibly up the aisle and married before we can fight ourselves free and run away."

Quite unexpectedly the *Duc* laughed.

"I do not believe I am hearing this," he said. "I have been pleaded with, pressured, and almost forced with a shot-gun at my back to say I would marry! Now you are telling me that the same thing is happening to you."

"Quite seriously, it is!" Marcia replied. "Papa has such an admiration for you that he thinks I must be mad when I say I will not marry you."

"I am sure your determination is very good for my soul," the *Duc* remarked, "but I feel it is somewhat deflating."

"Nonsense!" Marcia argued. "You are delighted at being 'let off the hook.' But I am quite certain you will find Papa and your Aunt the *Comtesse* very persuasive. The only thing we can do is to fight them together."

"There I agree with you," the *Duc* said, "and I am sure you are right in saying that it will not be easy."

"It is going to be difficult," Marcia agreed, "but if we can make it quite clear to them that neither of us has any intention of doing what they want, I shall be able to enjoy your horses without feeling embarrassed every time your Family look at me."

The *Duc* laughed again.

"I shall feel the same! We both know when we enter a room there will be a sudden silence as if they have been talking about us."

"They will do that," Marcia agreed, "so please, *Monsieur le Duc,* promise me that you will tell Papa very firmly, so that he cannot misunderstand, that you have no intention of proposing marriage to me."

"I promise!" the *Duc* said. "At the same time, I think this is the most extraordinary conversation I have ever had in the whole of my life!"

"Then that is settled," Marcia said. "Now I will race you to the end of the fields."

She did not wait for him to agree.

She pushed *Aquilin* forwards so quickly and so skilfully that she was some lengths away before the *Duc* realised what she was doing.

Then, as he followed her, he told himself that she was certainly the most extraordinary girl he had ever met.

And, from his point of view, quite the most sensible.

chapter five

THE *Duc* raced ahead of Marcia, and as they pulled in
their horses she was laughing.

She had no idea how lovely she looked with her eyes
sparkling, her cheeks flushed, and her golden hair rioting
over her head.

She turned to him and said:

"I am not going to say 'the best horse won,' because I
think your stallion is already very pleased with himself."

"And I suppose you are thinking the same of his
owner," the *Duc* remarked.

"But of course!" Marcia replied.

Looking towards the *Château* in the distance, she
added:

"How can you be anything else when you possess so
much of everything? But as my Nanny always warned
me: 'Pride comes before a fall!' "

"I think mine said something similar," the *Duc* said,
"but it would be churlish not to tell you that you
ride better than any woman I have ever seen."

"Papa would be pleased to hear that," Marcia answered.

Then she gave a little cry and put up her hand as if to silence her lips.

"Be careful! Be very careful!" she cried. "If you say anything like that to Papa, he will think that you are growing to like me."

She paused before she said urgently:

"I have just thought—nobody must know that we met out riding, and you must ignore me when we get back to the *Château*."

"Are you really telling me how to behave, Lady Marcia?" the *Duc* asked.

"Of course I am," Marcia replied. "I have as much, if not more, to lose than you by being a puppet in this ridiculous drama."

She did not see the surprise on the *Duc*'s face, but went on:

"The one thing we must not do is to ride back to the *Château* together. I will go one way, and you must go another."

"It gets more and more complicated," the *Duc* said, "but I understand what you are saying to me."

"I will hurry back now," Marcia said as if she were thinking it out, "and join Papa for breakfast. If you come in later, there is no need for anybody to think we met out riding."

She had assumed, as she spoke, that they had been unobserved.

Then she suddenly realised that it would not be difficult for some-one, if they were looking out of the windows, to be aware of them talking together.

Because the thought agitated her, she said quickly:

"I will go now, but before I do, may I choose which

horse I would like to ride this afternoon in the races?"

"No," the *Duc* replied, "I will choose one for you."

Marcia looked at him to see if he was serious and said:

"If it is some hobbledehoy animal which prevents me from winning any of the races, I shall get even with you in one way or another!"

She did not wait for his reply, but rode away on *Aquilin* at a gallop.

The *Duc* looked after her, thinking she was certainly amusing as well as being different from anyone else he had ever met.

Then, obediently, he turned his horse towards the valley.

He knew how he could arrive back at the *Château* by a different route from the one Marcia had taken.

* * *

Having left *Aquilin* in the stables, Marcia went into the *Château* to find her Father in the Breakfast-Room.

There were several other men there.

The majority of the women had either breakfasted in their bed-rooms or else it was still too early for them to appear.

Marcia did not mention that she had been out riding.

Her Father remarked as she kissed him good-morning:

"I see you are already dressed for the fray. I have been hearing more about the *Duc*'s exciting programme, and we must in one way or another keep the Union Jack flying."

"Of course we will, Papa," Marcia assured him.

The servants brought her several dishes to choose from.

This was different from the custom in England, where the guests helped themselves at breakfast-time from a selection of dishes on the sideboard.

She was hungry and found the salmon-trout which came from the river in the valley was delicious.

She was finishing her meal with toast and honey when the *Duc* came in.

"Good-morning, My Lord," he said to the Earl, and nodded to his friends around the table.

He ignored Marcia.

She saw her Father looked a little pained at the way he did so.

She quickly finished what she was eating and, rising, asked:

"What time will you be leaving for the paddocks, Papa?"

"I think we should follow the *Duc*'s instructions and go first to the stables," the Earl replied. "We will mount the horses we are to ride as we watch the parade."

"That is a good idea!" Marcia said.

"I will meet you in the Hall at a quarter past ten," the Earl went on, "and do not keep me waiting!"

"You know I am never late," Marcia replied.

She smiled at him and went from the room.

As she did so, one of the men at the table said:

"Your daughter, My Lord, is one of the most beautiful young women I have ever seen! You must be very proud of her."

It was a remark which the Earl had heard a thousand times, and he replied:

"Of course I am, and all I want is her future happiness."

He glanced, as he spoke, at the *Duc*, who was sitting down at the table.

He had, however, apparently not been listening to what was being said.

Upstairs Marcia changed into another habit which was the smartest she had brought with her.

She then arranged her hair, sweeping away the curls and making sure that it was smooth against her head.

Her riding-hat was exceedingly becoming with a gauze veil which fell down her back.

She was dressed entirely in the pale leaf-green of Spring.

When she came downstairs, all the women exclaimed at how smart she looked.

Only English Tailors, they said, could make riding-clothes which fitted so well.

Marcia went to the stables with her Father.

She found that he and she were privileged to be allowed to ride from the beginning of the proceedings.

The rest of the party were brought to the paddocks in an open Brake.

They were informed that they could not ride any of the horses until they had shown themselves off in the way the *Duc* had planned.

It was certainly a very impressive parade.

A groom or a stable-boy led every horse past the guests.

Their manes and tails had been decorated for the occasion.

Everybody applauded the outstanding stallions.

The *Duc* called out their names and gave the Earl and anyone else who wished to listen a short history of their breeding.

Marcia was fascinated.

She was also delighted with the horse she had been given by the Head Groom.

He was slightly larger than *Aquilin*.

She was sure the *Duc* would not have allowed any other woman in the party to ride him.

He was obstreperous and restless, but she soon had him under control.

As she did so, she had the idea that the *Duc* glanced at her approvingly.

She took care not to speak to him directly, and he did not speak to her.

But there was no necessity to look or think of anything but the horses themselves.

Then the races began.

They were joined by several of the *Duc*'s neighbours who wished to compete on their own horses.

Marcia lazily won the Ladies' Race, which took place first.

She was told that as the winner she could enter the Men's Race.

She had an idea it was something the *Duc* had thought up on the spur of the moment.

She could not help glancing at him with a grateful expression in her eyes.

It was clear from the twinkle in his that it was something he would not have allowed any other female rider to do.

Then quickly they looked away from each other in case anybody should be watching them.

The Men's Race on the flat was exciting.

Marcia came in fourth.

Later, after luncheon, she was allowed to enter the Steeple-Chase.

She knew then why the *Duc* had given her the particular horse she was riding.

While they had been inside the house, eating, and it

had been a very amusing meal, the fences had been erected on the Race-Course.

They were high, and after the first two or three the other women dropped out.

Finally the three leading horses were the *Duc*'s, Marcia's, and the Earl's.

It was a spectacular finish.

It was impossible to guess until the last moment who would be the winner.

Then, by a piece of superb riding, the *Duc* forged ahead and passed the Winning-Post a length ahead.

Marcia and her Father dead-heated.

She thought, as she pulled in her mount, that she had never enjoyed anything so much.

It was difficult not to enthuse with the *Duc*.

Her Father was able to tell him that he had never ridden a more satisfactory race.

By the time they returned to the *Château,* everybody was tired.

The ladies went to their bed-rooms to rest before dinner.

The *Comtesse* took Marcia to hers.

"You rode brilliantly, my dear," she said, "and I am sure my nephew must have been very impressed. There was no other woman present who could touch you."

"I had a very fine horse," Marcia said modestly. "And it was very, very exciting."

The *Comtesse* kissed her cheek.

"I am so glad you enjoyed it," she said. "I want you to be happy here at the *Château*."

Marcia was afraid she might say more.

To her relief, the maid came in to help her to remove her riding-clothes, and the *Comtesse* left.

They were a large party at dinner.

Afterwards there was a Band which played for them to dance.

The Ball-Room, as Marcia might have expected, was as exquisite as the rest of the house.

The white pillars picked out in gold were a perfect background.

It made the ladies in their beautiful gowns with their bustles and trains look like Swans.

The *Comtesse* and her contemporaries wore magnificent jewellery which glittered in the light of the chandeliers.

Marcia was besieged by partners, especially by the young men who had come from neighbouring houses.

At the same time, she could not help wishing that she could dance with the *Duc*.

Because he was so athletic, he moved round the Dance-Floor as elegantly as he rode his horses.

He deliberately avoided her.

She had, therefore, to content herself with peeping at him occasionally when she thought nobody else would be aware of it.

It was late when they went up to bed.

Some of the older guests, like her Father, had already retired.

Marcia was glad to put her head on the pillow and fell asleep almost immediately.

It had been a long day, but it had been a thrilling one.

* * *

Marcia was sailing over fences with several inches to spare when she awoke.

She thought at first that her maid must have called her.

Then she realised that her Father had come into the room and drawn back the curtains.

"I am sorry to wake you, my dear," he said, "but in a short while the *Duc* is taking me to visit one of his friends who has some particularly fine horses to sell, and he thought I might be interested."

"How exciting, Papa!" Marcia exclaimed, sitting up in bed and rubbing her eyes. "May I come too?"

"I wish you could, my Dearest," her Father answered, "but the *Duc* made it quite clear that the invitation was for me alone, and we are staying for luncheon."

"Oh . . . I understand."

As Marcia spoke, she thought the *Duc* was being sensible.

It would have caused comment if she had been included in the invitation.

However, she felt a little disappointed.

"What is the time, Papa?" she asked.

"Ten o'clock," the Earl replied.

Marcia gave a cry of dismay.

"I did not mean to sleep so late! I wanted to ride this morning."

"You will be able to do that after luncheon," the Earl said. "I do not expect we shall be back very early. The place to which we are going is some distance away."

He pulled up a chair to the bed and sat down.

"I woke you," he said, "because I want to talk to you."

"About what, Papa?" Marcia asked.

She put another pillow behind her head so that she could sit up.

As she faced her Father she wondered what he was about to say.

"I am afraid this will shock you, as indeed it has shocked me, but I think it is something you should know."

Marcia looked at him in surprise.

Then he told her exactly what the *Comtesse* had told him about Sardos.

Marcia listened.

Then, when her Father ceased speaking, she questioned:

"Do you really believe what the *Comtesse* has told you, Papa? It seems incredible!"

"That is what I thought myself," the Earl agreed. "At the same time, I dislike that young man, and I would not put anything past him."

"I dislike him too," Marcia agreed, "but it is difficult to believe that he would murder his Uncle."

"We cannot ignore the possibility," the Earl remarked.

"It is no concern of ours," Marcia said quietly.

The Earl was silent.

Then he said:

"I have always been very fond of the *Duc* since he was a small boy, and his Father was a friend of mine. Can I be so callous as to let this happen when I could prevent it?"

"You mean when *I* could prevent it by marrying the *Duc*!" Marcia contradicted. "But that would not stop Sardos trying to kill him, just because he was my husband."

"It would be a senseless murder—if you were having a child," the Earl said bluntly.

Marcia was still for a minute.

Then she said:

"Yes . . . of course . . . I had not . . . thought of that. But, surely, if at all, he will try to . . . murder the *Duc* before he is . . . married?"

"The *Comtesse* has begged the *Duc* to take every precaution. But you know as well as I do that if a man is determined to kill another, there are always opportunities which have not been anticipated. An unfortunate accident can always happen unexpectedly."

"It would be difficult to arrange one here," Marcia said, "when the *Duc* is surrounded by servants. But he would, of course, be wise not to ride alone, if that is what he does."

She thought, as she spoke, that it was foolish of the *Duc* to go out alone early in the morning.

If there was no guest to go with him, he could easily take a groom.

Yet she guessed it would annoy him to have to do so.

"I think," the Earl said slowly, "that what the *Duc* needs, and which might well save his life, is to have a wife to look after him."

Marcia gave a little cry and held up her hands.

"No, Papa, no! That may be your solution of throwing him a life-line, but it is not mine!"

The Earl rose from the chair.

"How can you be so stubborn and pig-headed?" he said in an exasperated tone. "What more could you want than this extremely prosperous Estate, this fine *Château*, and a man who, in my opinion, outshines and excels in every way all his contemporaries!"

There was a silence for a moment.

Then Marcia said quietly:

"You know perfectly well, Papa, that the *Duc* is not in love with me!"

"He might easily fall in love with you," the Earl said sharply, "if you were a little more pleasant to him. I noticed that you did not even congratulate him, when he won the race, and as far as I could see, you never spoke to him at any other time!"

"You could say he did not speak to *me!*" Marcia answered defiantly. "And you must be aware, Papa, that he is infatuated with the beautiful *Marquise,* even though he cannot marry her."

The Earl made a sound of disapproval.

"What is happening between the *Marquise* and the *Duc* is of no consequence. What is important to him and to his Family is that he should marry and produce a son."

He walked to the window.

"Can you imagine what will happen if that unpleasant young man Sardos inherits the Estate when his Mother dies?"

He put his hand down heavily on the window sill and said:

"Long before she is dead he will have sold everything he can get hold of to spend on the prostitutes of Paris. He will strip the *Château* bare of everything in it that has been accumulated over the centuries."

"You make it sound very sad, Papa. However, I am not concerned with what happens to the *Château,* but with the happiness I have found at home at Woode Hall and the possessions which you have told me will be mine one day."

"If that is your attitude," the Earl said angrily, "there is no point in our going on talking about it."

"None at all, Papa," Marcia agreed. "I am sorry for the *Duc,* but his troubles are not mine. There are plenty of attractive girls in France who would do everything in their power to save him if he so much as raised his little finger."

The Earl did not answer.

He walked out of the bed-room and slammed the door behind him.

Marcia sighed.

She hated upsetting her Father, whom she loved.

At the same time, she was convinced that he was exaggerating the whole situation.

He was only using it as a lever to force her into marrying the *Duc*.

She wondered if he had said anything to the *Duc* himself.

She longed to know what was happening, but thought it would be very difficult to have another private conversation with him.

'Perhaps to-morrow morning I shall have a chance,' she thought.

She determined to rise early, as she had yesterday, and go riding at six o'clock.

She thought she would try to convey to him by some means that that was what she intended to do.

The question was how she would get the opportunity.

Because she had no wish to see her Father again before he left, she did not come downstairs until it was nearly midday.

The *Comtesse* greeted her profusely.

"Here you are, Dearest Child," she said. "I trust you are rested?"

"I am afraid I am very late, *Madame,*" Marcia apologised.

"We all were," the *Comtesse* replied, "but there was every excuse, and fortunately my nephew did not want an audience to-day. As I expect you know, he has taken your Father off to see some horses."

"I know that will be delightful for Papa," Marcia replied.

Most of the men in the party seemed to have vanished for one reason or another.

Marcia found the luncheon was a dull meal compared to those she had enjoyed before.

As soon as they had finished, the *Comtesse* was called away to deal with some problem which concerned the House-hold.

Marcia had no wish to talk with the other relatives in the *Salon*.

She was afraid they would start trying to pump her as to what she felt about the *Duc*.

She was sure they were longing to find out if she was in love with him or not.

Marcia told herself with a little smile that if she told them the truth, they would find it unbelievable.

She therefore went upstairs and put on a riding-skirt and her thin blouse.

Then she slipped down a side staircase which led to the stables.

She asked the grooms if she could ride *Aquilin*, and the Head Groom remarked:

"I'm sure, *Mademoiselle,* you'd wish for a groom to accompany you."

"No, thank you," Marcia replied. "I would much rather go alone."

She saw by the expression on the groom's face that he disapproved of her doing so.

She understood that in the early morning, when there was nobody about, it might be proper to ride without an attendant.

But it would be considered correct to have a groom with her at any other time of the day.

She wanted to think over what her Father had said.

She had no wish to have a groom either talking or keeping just behind her wherever she went.

Whether or not the Head Groom approved, she had

every intention of being alone.

He brought *Aquilin* to the mounting-block.

As she left, he watched with a disapproving look in his eyes.

However, she had got her own way.

She set off, moving along the gorges which she wanted to explore more closely.

She had not gone far when she got a small fly in her eye.

She pulled *Aquilin* to a standstill under the boughs of some trees.

Having managed to extract the small insect, she wiped her eye with her handkerchief.

As she did so, she saw ahead of her two men apparently coming out from one of the gorges.

She could not see them very clearly, but she was sure one of them was Sardos.

He had not been at luncheon, and the *Comtesse* had said:

"I am afraid, and it is rather disillusioning, but all the men have left us on one pretext or another."

There was a little murmur from the women as the *Comtesse* went on:

"Even Sardos said he had business to do, but I cannot imagine what it could be, here in the valley."

There was a worried note in her voice.

It made Marcia think she was speaking more to herself than to those listening.

Now, as she saw Sardos riding along with the other man beside, she wondered if he was up to some mischief.

It seemed unlikely that there was anything here he could do to hurt the *Duc*.

He would not find money amongst the high rocks, nor,

for that matter, in the valley, as the grapes were not yet ripe for picking.

She waited until the two men were out of sight.

Then she rode on, keeping still close to the magnificent rocks.

They rose on one side of her, high up towards the sky.

Then she was aware that in front of her was a hedge.

It was quite a high one, but it seemed to be a challenge.

She bent forward to pat *Aquilin* on the neck.

"Come on, boy," she said in French. "Show me what you can do."

She put him at the hedge and he swept over it with almost a foot to spare.

As they were flying over it, Marcia realised with a sense of shock that there was a child on the other side.

She only just had time to pull *Aquilin* over to the right.

He reacted, but not enough.

As he landed, one of his back hoofs just touched the child, and she fell to the ground.

Marcia leapt from the saddle and ran towards the fallen child.

She was a little girl of perhaps five years of age.

She had been holding a bunch of wild flowers in her hand which she had been picking from beneath the hedgerows.

Marcia picked the child up in her arms and looked round wildly.

It was then she saw that about fifty yards away to her left there was a small house.

It was at the foot of the towering rocks.

She started to walk towards it.

As she did so, a boy who appeared to be about fourteen years old came running towards her.

"What's happened?" he asked.

"Who is this little girl?" Marcia enquired.

"She's m'sister, Lisette," the boy answered. "Mama told me to look after her. Is she dead?"

"No, of course not," Marcia replied quickly. "She was just touched by my horse's hoof and it has knocked her unconscious."

She hoped, as she spoke, that it was nothing more serious that that.

Still walking forward, she said to the boy:

"Is that your home? Is your Mother there?"

"M'Mother's gone to see Grandpapa, who's ill," the boy answered.

Marcia felt her heart sink.

She could see the house was standing by itself and there was no sign of any others.

Still she walked on, holding the child very carefully.

She looked at her and could see now that she was a pretty little girl.

Aquilin's hoof had caught her in the centre of her forehead.

Only a little of the skin was broken and it was not bleeding profusely.

But already a dark patch was forming round it which looked ominous.

The boy was obviously very perturbed.

"What'll you do?" he asked. "Will Lisette be in great pain?"

"I hope not," Marcia answered, "but we must get a Doctor to her as soon as possible."

The boy shook his head.

"There's no Doctor near here."

Marcia knew she must find somebody to help her.

'I will send a message to the *Château*,' she thought.

They had reached the house, which had a small garden in front of it.

The boy opened the gate.

There was a narrow path leading up to the front-door which he ran ahead to open.

Before Marcia went inside she looked back.

To her relief, *Aquilin* was cropping the grass near the hedge.

She doubted if he would wander away.

If he did, it was more than likely that he would return to his own stable.

For the moment, however, she must concern herself with Lisette.

The house was very small, with a kitchen on one side of the front-door and a Parlour on the other.

At the back were two bed-rooms.

In the larger of these there was a big bed and a smaller one which the boy said was Lisette's.

Marcia, however, put the child down on the big bed.

Her eyes were still closed and her face was very white.

Because she was frightened, Marcia found that her heart was beating abnormally quickly.

"Your little sister is concussed," she said aloud, "and we must get help. You must run to the *Château* with a note."

The boy nodded in understanding and she asked:

"What is your name?"

"It's Pierre."

"Very well, Pierre," Marcia said. "See if you can find me a piece of paper, some ink, and a pen with which to write. I will undress your sister, but tell me first where I can find her nightgown."

The boy picked up the pillow from Lisette's bed and from beneath it drew out a nightgown.

Marcia saw that it was clean, as were the bed-clothes and the house itself.

She thought Pierre's Mother must be a competent housewife.

Then she remembered that the French were always excessively clean in their own houses.

They aired their mattresses almost every day out of the windows.

"Find me some paper to write on," she said again.

Pierre disappeared.

Marcia went to the wash-hand-stand in the corner of the room.

There was a ewer filled with water and she found a flannel hanging on the towel-rail.

Very gently she bathed Lisette's forehead.

There was a little blood, but not much.

Marcia thought, however, that the bruise caused by *Aquilin*'s hoof had grown bigger and blacker.

She took off Lisette's shoes and socks.

She was just beginning to undo her cotton dress when Pierre came back.

"I have found some ink and a quill, *M'mselle,*" he said, "also a piece o' paper, but it's a bit large."

It was a piece which Marcia thought his Mother must have used on the kitchen-table.

She had seen a pair of scissors on the dressing-table, and she cut it down to the size she wanted.

Then she seated herself in a hard chair.

Dipping the quill in the ink-pot, she wrote:

I have had an accident involving a small child. Please send a Doctor or somebody to help, but do not tell anybody in the house about it, especially Papa, as it would upset and worry him. Marcia.

She folded the note, hoping that no-one would open it.

Then she wrote on the outside the *Duc*'s name and above it PRIVATE AND PERSONAL.

When she had finished, she said to Pierre:

"Take this as quickly as you can to the *Château* and say it is for the *Duc* and nobody else. Try, if it is possible, to give it to him yourself."

The boy understood and Marcia said:

"Be as quick as you can, but tell me before you go when your Mother will be back."

"She said perhaps very late to-night," he answered, "but she thought more likely it'd be to-morrow morning."

Marcia's heart sank.

"Do everything you can to speak to *Monsieur le Duc* himself," she said. "He will help us while other people will only make a fuss."

"I'll say that I come from you, *M'mselle*," Pierre said intelligently, "if you'll tell me your name."

Marcia thought it was clever of him to think of that.

"I am Lady Marcia Woode," she said. "Repeat that after me."

"I . . . Lady Marcia Woode," Pierre repeated, having a little difficulty with the word "Lady."

"That is right," Marcia said. "Now repeat it to me and then over and over to yourself as you run to the *Château*."

He did as she told him and ran off, saying:

"I'm a good runner, *M'mselle*. I'll be very quick!"

Marcia went to the door with him and looked to see that *Aquilin* was still there.

The horse was apparently quite unconcerned by what was happening.

108

With a faint sense of relief she went back to Lisette.

The child had not moved.

Very gently Marcia began to take off her dress, thinking that once she regained consciousness she would be more comfortable without it.

At the same time, she was frightened by what had happened.

Perhaps the child's brain had been damaged by the accident.

'I am sure the *Duc* will find a Doctor,' she thought.

She only hoped he had returned by now.

She hoped he and her Father would have seen the horses before luncheon and would not linger too long afterwards.

"Only the *Duc* can help me at this moment," she told herself.

Then she thought it was strange that she should rely on him so completely.

chapter six

PIERRE ran all the way to the *Château*.

He was breathless when he got there.

Then, as he reached the steps to the front-door, he felt shy at what he had to do.

He glanced back down the drive and saw that a Chaise was approaching.

He stopped, thinking perhaps it was the *Duc*.

If it was, he would not have to speak to the superior footmen, who frightened him.

The Chaise came nearer.

The *Duc* was driving two well-matched horses, which he brought to a standstill with a flourish.

Pierre saw the gentleman with him get out.

As the *Duc* was about to hand the reins to the groom who had been perched up behind, Pierre stepped forward.

"I 'ave this for you, *Monsieur*," Pierre said, bowing.

He held out the note which Marcia had written to him.

The *Duc* looked at the boy in surprise.

"A note for me?" he asked. "From whom?"

"From *M'mselle-Ladee-Marcia-Woode,*" Pierre answered slowly, struggling to remember the words.

The *Duc* took the note from him and opened it.

When he had read it, he asked:

"Where is the lady who wrote this?"

"In m'Mother's cottage, *Monsieur.*"

"Wait here," the *Duc* said.

He walked up the steps into the Hall and said to one of the footmen:

"Fetch Jacques to me immediately."

"Oui, Monsieur," the footman replied, and ran up the stairs.

The Earl had moved through the Hall and into the *Salon*.

The *Duc* could hear his voice talking, he thought, to the *Comtesse*.

He waited impatiently.

He had decided it would be a mistake to speak of what the note contained until he had found out what had happened.

It was only a few minutes before Jacques, the *Duc*'s Valet, came hurrying down the stairs.

He was a middle-aged man who had been with the *Duc* for ten years.

He was extremely skilful in rendering first-aid in accidents.

The *Duc* had incurred a number in his various exploits.

He drew Jacques out of hearing of the other servants and, speaking in a low voice, said:

"There has been an accident and I want you to come with me at once. Bring anything you think might be necessary."

Jacques did not waste any time in asking questions.

He merely ran back up the stairs while the *Duc* walked to the front-door.

"Tell the Earl and the *Comtesse* if they ask for me," he said to the Butler, "that I have gone to see somebody on the Estate who needs my help."

As the *Duc* finished speaking, he walked down the steps and got back into his Chaise.

The groom was standing at the horses' heads.

The *Duc* waited until Jacques came hurrying back to join him.

As the Valet got into the Chaise, the *Duc* said to the groom:

"I am going only a short distance, so I will not need you any longer."

The groom stood back and the *Duc* said to Pierre, who stood waiting:

"Get into the seat behind me."

At his command Pierre quickly obeyed.

The *Duc* turned the horses in the Court-yard and set off down the drive.

He waited until he was out of sight of the house before he said, speaking over his shoulder, to Pierre:

"You will have to direct me. I have no idea where your cottage is."

Pierre told him that they must pass through the village first.

Having done so, they then took a rough track up the hillside.

It was fortunate there had been no rain, for the last part of the journey meant driving across the fields over which Marcia had been riding.

As they neared the cottage, the *Duc* saw *Aquilin*, who was still cropping the grass.

He looked apprehensively at the horse, wondering if he should tie him up or leave him as he was.

Aquilin raised his head as the Chaise approached.

He made no effort to move away. The *Duc* thought it would be safe to leave him loose.

He got out, saying to Pierre as he did so:

"I am leaving my horses in your charge, and I know you will look after them."

He knew he could not have said anything which delighted the boy more.

He ran to the horses' heads and started to make a fuss of them.

The *Duc* opened the gate, went up the narrow path, and entered the cottage.

He guessed immediately where Marcia would be.

It was only a few steps to the bed-room at the back, and when he reached it he saw that the door was ajar.

He pushed it open and saw Marcia sitting on the bed, cradling Lisette in her arms.

She did not know immediately that the *Duc* was there.

She was talking to the child, and he could hear her saying in her soft voice:

"You have been hurt, but you will soon be well. Then you will be able to run over the grass again and pick the pretty flowers as you did to-day. I expect you were going to give them to your Mother, and she will be pleased that you thought of her while she was away."

She was suddenly aware that there was somebody at the door and looked up to see the *Duc*.

"You . . . you have come!" she said in a different tone. "I am so glad! I have been so worried. Have you brought a Doctor with you?"

"I have brought my Valet, Jacques, who is just as good as any Doctor," the *Duc* replied. "What has happened?"

He walked nearer to the bed and looked down at the child in Marcia's arms.

"It was . . . my fault," she said unhappily. "I jumped a hedge without knowing there was anyone on the other side. One of *Aquilin*'s hoofs just touched this child's forehead. I think she is concussed and I hope it is no worse than that."

"We will let Jacques take a look at her," the *Duc* said.

He stood aside while Jacques, who had been hovering at the door, came forward.

He looked down at Lisette, and Marcia said:

"I think it is a good sign that the wound has not bled much, but she is going to have a terrible bruise on her forehead."

Jacques took Lisette's pulse and felt her heart, and then very gently her forehead.

"How is she?" Marcia asked. "I was so afraid at first that she was dead."

"Do not worry, *M'mselle,*" Jacques said as he smiled. "The little girl is very much alive but, as you said, she has concussion. I do not think, however, that her head is seriously hurt."

"Are you going to bandage it?" Marcia asked.

The Valet shook his head.

"I never bandage wounds if I can avoid it. I prefer to use the clean air and the sunshine of *le Bon Dieu,* which heals far better than anything else."

Marcia smiled at him.

"That is what my Mother used to say. She was also a great believer in honey."

"As I am, *M'mselle,*" Jacques agreed. "I have here a cream which I make myself from honey. It will heal the cut quicker than anything a Doctor could prescribe."

He opened the bag he had brought with him and took out a pot.

Gently he applied the cream to the bruise that was getting darker every moment, and the broken skin.

"Now," he said, "all you have to do is to keep her quiet and not let her be frightened when she wakes."

The *Duc*, who until now had been silent, moved to the bed.

"Where is the child's Mother?" he asked. "Surely she will be home soon, if she is working in the field."

"She has had to go away, perhaps for the night," Marcia replied, "but she will return to-morrow morning. I will look after Lisette until then."

The *Duc* looked at her in surprise.

"You mean you intend to stay here?" he asked. "Would you not prefer to bring the child back to the *Château*?"

"No, no," Marcia said quickly. "I am sure she would be frightened unless, when she regains consciousness, she is at home."

"And you are going to stay here with her?" the *Duc* asked as if he could hardly believe what he had heard.

He could not imagine any other woman of his acquaintance staying in a peasant's cottage to look after a sick child she had never seen before.

"Of course I must stay," Marcia replied. "It is my fault that she is in this condition and . . . she is such a pretty little girl."

"You must do as you see fit," the *Duc* agreed, "but I do not think you will be at all comfortable."

Marcia did not bother to answer him.

She was holding the child close against her breast.

Although she was no longer speaking to Lisette, the *Duc* had the feeling that she was willing her to consciousness.

"Where is the child's Father?" he asked.

There was silence, as if it took a little time for his question to penetrate Marcia's mind.

"I . . . I never thought to ask Pierre," she replied.

The *Duc* walked out of the bed-room.

Jacques put the pot containing the honey down on a table and added some other things to it.

Pierre was with the horses, patting and making a fuss of them.

The *Duc* went to his side.

"Where is your Father?" he asked.

"My Father's dead, *Monsieur,*" Pierre answered. "He was killed by a rock-fall last Winter."

"How does your Mother manage without him?" the *Duc* questioned.

"She takes in washing for some of the people in the village," Pierre explained, "and makes lace which she sells in the Market."

The *Duc* was aware that the local lace was much in demand by the tourists, and many ladies found a use for it.

"And you do not think your Mother will be back to-night?"

Pierre gave a shrug of his shoulders.

"If Grandpapa's better she'll come back to-night, *Monsieur.* If not, very early to-morrow morning."

Having found out what he wanted to know, the *Duc* went back to the house.

Jacques was just coming out of the bed-room.

The *Duc* took him into the kitchen and gave him a number of instructions.

Jacques listened intently to what he had to say before he replied:

"I will arrange it, *Monsieur.*"

"Thank you, Jacques," the *Duc* said. "Now, while you drive the Chaise back to the *Château*, I will attend to *Aquilin*."

"I saw him in the field, *Monsieur*. It is a good thing that he was not hurt."

"That is what I thought myself," the *Duc* replied.

Jacques got into the Chaise and drove off.

The *Duc* walked over to *Aquilin*, who nuzzled against him.

He tied the reins on his neck, which Marcia had omitted to do, and led him to the cottage.

"Now, be a good boy and do not go too far," the *Duc* said.

He walked to where Pierre was standing at the gate, watching him.

"Keep an eye on my horse," the *Duc* said. "I would be very upset if I lost him."

"I'll look after him, *Monsieur*," Pierre said eagerly.

"You do that, and I will give you something to spend in the village," the *Duc* promised.

He saw the boy's eyes light up.

He guessed that since his Father had died, his Mother was finding it difficult to feed her children and herself on what she earned.

Marcia looked up in surprise as the *Duc* came back into the bed-room.

"You are still here!" she exclaimed. "I heard horses' hoofs and thought you had gone back to the *Château*."

"I am afraid if I return I shall be bombarded with questions as to what has happened," the *Duc* replied.

Marcia gave a little laugh.

"That is something which is certain to happen! I am . . . very ashamed of what I have done."

"There is no need to be."

"I will never forgive myself if I have really hurt . . . this child," Marcia went on, "but your Valet, Jacques, thinks the injury is not a serious one and her brain has not been . . . damaged."

"I have trusted Jacques with my body and my brain for many years," the *Duc* said, "and he has never failed me."

He was noticing, as he spoke, how very tenderly Marcia was looking at Lisette and how lovingly she held her.

Marcia had taken off her riding-boots when she sat on the bed.

Now she was propped up against the pillows.

She was looking exceedingly lovely as she bent her golden head over the unconscious child.

The *Duc* sat down in a chair and watched her.

Because he was silent, Marcia looked up at him enquiringly.

"I think you are very fond of children," he said.

"I love them," Marcia answered, "and because I was an only child I longed to have brothers and sisters with whom I could play."

She looked down at Lisette again before she went on:

"It has, of course, been wonderful to be with Papa, although he always treated me as if I were his son rather than his daughter. But I want my daughter, if I have one, to play with dolls and to think of them, as I wanted to do, as if they were her children."

She was speaking in a dreamlike voice, as if to herself.

"If you feel like that," the *Duc* said, "why do you not get married and have children of your own?"

"That is what I would like to do when I find a man who would care for them as much as I do," Marcia replied.

119

The *Duc* thought this over. Then he said:

"What you are saying is that the men who have proposed to you, and I gather there have been a great number, would not, in your opinion, have made good Fathers."

"They might have done," Marcia admitted, "but they gave no indication of it. And how could I bring children into the world who might be neglected or feel they were unwanted?"

She was still speaking in a low, quiet voice.

The *Duc* realised it was not only because she thought it might disturb the unconscious child.

It was also because for the moment she had forgotten who he was, or that he was being rather impertinent in asking her such questions.

He though, however, that what she was saying was very revealing.

Because he was very astute, he had learned what nobody else had—the secret of Marcia's aversion to an arranged marriage, or any marriage that was not one of love.

As if she were suddenly aware of what he was thinking, she looked up at him.

"You will not tell anybody what I have just said to you?"

"You can trust me," the *Duc* replied, "and if it interests you, I can tell you that I too was very lonely when I was a child."

"It is different for boys," she said as if she did not want to be sympathetic.

The *Duc* shook his head.

"I think all children need the same things—companionship and, of course, love."

"I cannot believe that your Mother did not love you," Marcia remarked.

120

"She loved me and so did my Father," the *Duc* replied, "but I still told myself stories in which I had another boy of my own age with whom I could climb trees, hide from my Nurses and Tutors, and who, of course, raced me on my pony whenever I went riding."

Marcia gave a little laugh.

"I wanted that too, and I felt it was unfair that Papa always won because he was on a much larger horse than I was."

"I often thought," the *Duc* went on as if he were looking back into the past, "that the village children, who nearly all came from large Families, were happier than I was playing alone in the huge Nurseries of the *Château* with every expensive toy that had ever been invented."

"Now you are making me feel sorry for you," Marcia said, "and I want to feel sorry for Lisette because I have hurt her, and also because she must be a lonely child, as Pierre is so much older than she is."

"I have a half-sister, but she is twelve years older than I," the *Duc* remarked.

"Then obviously the best thing you can do," Marcia said, "is to have a large Family of your own. Make certain that you have them close together—as twins if possible—so that they will never feel lonely."

As she spoke she remembered—she had forgotten it until now—what her Father had told her.

If he was right in what he had said, there was every possibility that the *Duc* would marry no-one.

The Nurseries at the *Château* would remain empty.

Without thinking that he might not know of Sardos's intentions, she said quickly:

"You must be careful . . . very careful! Otherwise there will be no more *Duc*s de Roux, and certainly no children to slide down the banisters and play *Hide-*

and-Seek in those exciting corridors."

"What are you talking about?" the *Duc* asked.

"I . . . I am sorry . . . I should not have mentioned it," Marcia replied. "It was . . . stupid of me . . . but I thought *Madame la Comtesse* must have warned you."

"Warned me? About what?" the *Duc* enquired.

"About . . . your nephew."

"Is there anything new about him that I have not heard?"

"I . . . I do not know . . . but Papa told me something this morning."

"Tell me what your Father told you."

Marcia looked up at the *Duc* with a worried expression in her eyes.

"It was . . . tactless of me to mention it . . . please . . . forget what I just said."

"You cannot expect me not to be curious!"

She gave a sigh.

"It will come much better from the *Comtesse* than from me, but . . . she thinks that your nephew intends to . . . murder you!"

The *Duc* stared at her.

"Murder me?" he exclaimed. "But that is ridiculous!"

"Apparently the Count told his Creditors that when you . . . died, which you were likely to do in the . . . near future, his Mother would inherit . . . everything you . . . possess."

There was silence.

Because she was shy, Marcia did not look up at the *Duc*.

She bent over Lisette, her head bowed so that he could see only the top of it.

"What you have just said about his Mother is true," the *Duc* said after what seemed a long silence. "I was not aware that Sardos would scheme to use it to his advantage."

"It would be very much to his advantage," Marcia answered, "if he could dispose of you in some way. Oh, please . . . please . . . be careful! You cannot let somebody . . . like him take your place . . . I am quite certain that all the people on the Estate . . . including Pierre and Lisette's Mother . . . would suffer if he . . . did."

"Of course they would," the *Duc* answered, "but I had no idea he was desperate enough to be prepared to murder me!"

"It is only . . . an idea," Marcia said quickly. "No-one can be certain of it, except that the *Comtesse* has been in touch with some friends in Paris who say he is deliberately making it known that his Mother will benefit by your death."

"Which is something that must certainly be avoided at all costs," the *Duc* said grimly.

He got up from the chair in which he was sitting, walked to the door, and left the room.

Marcia looked after him with an anxious expression in her eyes.

'Perhaps I should not have told him,' she thought, 'but he will have to know sooner or later that he must take better care of . . . himself.'

It was then she remembered having seen Sardos with a companion riding not far from where they were at this moment.

They might have been doing nothing wrong and were just out for a ride.

But she thought that if she were the *Duc*, she would be suspicious of everything Sardos did and everywhere he went.

Suddenly she found herself praying that the *Duc*

would be safe and no-one would harm him.

She felt if he was murdered it would be like some great oak falling to the ground, or the *Château* crumbling in pieces.

* * *

The *Duc,* as it happened, was standing at the front-door, looking out onto the valley.

Was it really possible, he asked himself, that his nephew would murder him because he needed more money for his wild extravagances?

He told himself the idea was absurd.

He refused to be intimidated, even in his thoughts, by somebody so despicable.

But he could not bear to think of all his work on the vines, all the innovations he had introduced, being squandered on drink and immoral women.

'I suppose,' he thought finally, 'I shall have to give Sardos some more money, although, God knows, I might as well throw it down the drain!'

He was still standing at the door when Jacques arrived back.

He was driving a cart drawn by only one horse and moving very quickly.

When the *Duc* saw him coming across the rough ground, he smiled.

He knew he could trust Jacques to carry out his instructions to the very letter.

Jacques stopped the cart at the gate and beckoned to Pierre.

The boy was still standing near *Aquilin.*

"Come and help me," the Valet said. "I have a lot of things to carry into your Mother's kitchen."

Curious as to what they could be, Pierre was delighted to help him.

The *Duc* went back into the bed-room.

"Jacques has returned," he said to Marcia. "As you are determined to stay here, he has brought you some night-attire so that you will be more comfortable."

"How kind of you to think of it," she replied. "After your Valet had gone, I was, in fact, wishing I could take off my riding-skirt, as it is rather hot."

"That is what I suggest you do now," the *Duc* said, "so I will fetch what Jacques has brought."

He went out to the cart and picked up a small suit-case.

He took it into the bed-room.

Marcia had already got off the bed and put Lisette very carefully down with her head on the pillow.

She was standing on the floor and bending over the little girl as the *Duc* entered.

As he watched her, he thought she might have posed for a great Master's portrait of *The Virgin and Child*.

"Here is your suit-case," he said, "and I am certain, knowing Jacques, that nothing has been forgotten."

"Please thank him for me," Marcia answered, "and I am so grateful to be able to change into something cooler."

The *Duc* went away, shutting the door behind him.

Marcia slipped off her riding-skirt and the clothes she wore under it.

When she opened the suit-case she found that Jacques had brought her one of her pretty nightgowns and a negligee.

If was of white satin trimmed with little bows of sky-blue velvet.

She had brought it because it was so pretty.

But she had certainly not expected to wear it in a peasant's cottage.

Jacques had also included her hair-brush, comb, and a travelling-mirror.

It was much more convenient that the very small mirror attached to a wooden frame on the dressing-table.

Marcia loosened her hair and brushed it until it seemed to come to life with the electricity in it.

It fell over her shoulders nearly to her waist.

She shut her suit-case, having found a pair of heel-less slippers.

It amused her to find that Jacques had also put in the book she had been reading, which had been on her bed-side table.

It would help to pass an hour or two, she thought, until she could fall asleep.

There was a knock on the door.

She thought it must be Pierre, but when she called out *"Entrez"* it was the *Duc* who stood there.

"I thought you had gone!" she said.

"On the contrary," he replied, "I am waiting for you to have Dinner with me."

Marcia stared at him.

"Dinner?"

"It would hardly be hospitable if, as your Host, I left you here with nothing to eat."

"I thought there might be something in the kitchen," Marcia replied.

"It would be very little," the *Duc* said, "and Jacques has brought what he thought we would both enjoy."

Marcia laughed.

"I do not believe it! What will they think at the *Château* when you do not appear at Dinner?"

"I have told Jacques to say that I am dining with friends, and that you have gone to their house for help because *Aquilin* had cast a shoe, and while the Blacksmith is re-shoeing the horse you are dining there too."

"How can you make up such a lot of lies?" Marcia asked.

But she was laughing.

" 'Needs must when the Devil drives!' " the *Duc* replied. "Now come into the Parlour, and let me tell you, in case you are worried, that Pierre is eating like a horse at the kitchen-table! If you do not hurry, there will be nothing left for us!"

Marcia laughed again, then she looked anxiously towards Lisette.

"We can leave the door open," the *Duc* said, "so that if she regains consciousness or moves, we will hear her."

Marcia gave him a little smile before she walked ahead of him into the small Parlour.

It was a tiny room, sparsely furnished, but spotlessly clean.

Jacques had arranged a table in the centre of the room.

There was a lace-edged tablecloth and two silver candlesticks which he had brought from the *Château*.

Marcia sat down and the *Duc* sat opposite her.

Their first course was already on the table.

There were slices of the delicious *Pâté de foie gras*, which was a speciality of that part of the Dordogne.

There was champagne to drink.

As Marcia sipped it, she said:

"I only hope that nobody at the *Château* has any idea of where we are at the moment. Can you imagine how shocked they would be!"

"We are eating together without a chaperon," the *Duc* said, "and you look very lovely with your hair down and wearing your night-attire."

"It is a *négligée*," Marcia commented, "and you are well aware that a lady can wear that when she receives a *Beau* in her *Boudoir*."

"You are making that sound even more improper than it is!" the *Duc* teased.

Marcia blushed, realising that she had spoken as she might have done to her Father.

She had forgotten that the *Duc* was a young man and she should have been more formal with him.

"I like it when you blush," the *Duc* remarked. "It is something I seldom see on a Frenchwoman's face."

He thought, as he spoke, that it was not surprising.

The women with whom he associated, like the *Marquise,* had years ago passed the age of blushing.

"As we are here in such compromising circumstances," Marcia said quickly, "I suggest we talk about horses, which is always a safe subject."

"I would, at the moment, rather talk about you!" the *Duc* said firmly. "I was extremely interested in what you said just now about being an only child. While I was waiting for you to change, I was thinking how much the *Château* and the Estate have meant to me ever since I can remember. And therefore how important it is that it should go to my son, or perhaps several sons."

Marcia clapped her hands.

"That is what everyone has wanted you to think," she said, "and nobody could be more delighted than your Aunt."

"The difficulty is," the *Duc* went on, "that, as you said yourself, to have children you must have love, and if the home is to be the right sort for them, whether it is as small as this cottage or as big as the *Château*, their Father and Mother must love each other."

"You are absolutely right in saying that," Marcia said seriously. "I am convinced that children born of love are more intelligent and, of course, much happier than those who are not."

The *Duc* nodded, and she went on:

"If you read History, it is obvious that love-children were always very much cleverer than those born of arranged marriages, especially those that were Royal."

"That is true," the *Duc* agreed, "and I can prove to you by many examples that the love-children of many a French King excelled in every way those born to his foreign Bride for whom he had little or no affection."

"We have exactly the same experience in English History," Marcia agreed.

She told him stories of several Royal love-children.

Then the *Duc* told her similar stories of those born to French Kings, which she found fascinating.

The *Pâté* was followed by a number of delicious dishes brought in by Jacques.

But they were so engrossed in their conversation that they ate with no attention to the food.

Marcia hardly even tasted the superb wine which came from the *Duc*'s own Vineyard.

Finally, after they had had coffee, the *Duc* rose reluctantly.

"And now, I suppose, I must return to the *Château*. I will tell your Father the truth of what has happened, but I think it would be a mistake for my Aunt, or anybody else, to know."

"Oh, please . . . keep it a secret!" Marcia begged. "You know how they would talk, and it would be very, very embarrassing for me."

"I will do my best," the *Duc* promised, "and of course I will come back early to-morrow morning to collect you when the child's Mother has arrived."

The *Duc* moved a few steps towards the door before he said:

"Good-night, Marcia. I have enjoyed our dinner

together more than I can possibly say."

"And I found it fascinating," Marcia answered. "Good-night, *Monsieur*, and . . . thank you."

The *Duc* took her hand in his.

Then, to her surprise, his lips touched the softness of her skin.

He walked into the kitchen to see if Jacques was ready.

Marcia, however, hurried to the bed-room to see if Lisette was all right.

The child lay just where she had left her.

Gently she lifted her as she turned down the covers and slid her into the large bed.

She was a little apprehensive as to whether the sheets would be clean.

To her relief she found they had never been slept in and must have been changed that very morning.

Before getting into bed she went to the window to open it a little wider.

Jacques had lit two candles for her which stood on the dressing-table.

They were similar to those that had been on the Dining-Room table.

She was sure they were very much more expensive than a Cottager could afford.

It was then she saw something lying on the dressing-table which had not been there before.

It was a revolver.

She wondered why Jacques had put it there, then realised that beneath it was a note:

Mademoiselle,
   I heard to-day there is in the vicinity a dog with rabies. The Valet of Monsieur the Earl of Grateswoode tells me you are a good shot. I am

therefore leaving this for you in case of trouble.

> *Yours respectfully,*
> *Jacques.*

Marcia smiled, thinking he was a very intelligent man.

She knew how dangerous a dog with rabies could be.

At the same time, she hoped she would not have to shoot it.

She pulled one of the curtains over, then looked up at the sky.

It seemed far away because behind the cottage were the hard rocks rising up for hundreds of feet.

By throwing back her head she could see just above them that dusk was falling and the first evening stars were twinkling.

It was very beautiful.

She was thinking that she would go to the front of the house and look at the valley in the moonlight.

She knew that Jacques had left by now, as she had heard the wheels.

She was aware without asking that the *Duc* would return to the *Château* on *Aquilin*.

She could imagine how magnificent he would look.

'It was very kind of him to have Dinner with me,' she thought, 'and I so much enjoyed our conversation.'

She only hoped he had not been too bored.

He certainly had seemed to be amused and interested.

She pulled the curtain to and blew out one of the candles.

She was just putting the other beside her bed when her door was suddenly flung open.

"M'mselle! M'mselle," a voice cried.

It was Pierre, and she put down the candle, saying:

"What is it, Pierre? What has happened?"

131

"They've taken *Monsieur le Duc* prisoner, *M'mselle!* Three men have taken him into the cave."

"I do not know what you are saying!" Marcia exclaimed.

"They put a rope round him. He struggled, but they were too strong for him," Pierre said breathlessly. "They knocked off his hat and he fought them, *M'mselle,* but they dragged him into the big cave which no one knows about except my friend and me!"

Marcia knew it was Sardos.

She could only think with horror that he would kill the *Duc.*

chapter seven

"WHAT . . . can we . . . do?" Marcia gasped.

"I'll show you without them seeing us," Pierre said, "where they have taken *Monsieur le Duc*. Come with me, *M'mselle*."

Marcia looked quickly at Lisette, who was lying still.

Then she turned towards the door where Pierre was waiting for her.

It was then she remembered the revolver which Jacques had left for her lying on the dressing-table.

She picked it up, then she realised that Pierre had gone ahead.

She found him coming from the kitchen, carrying something in his hands.

"I've a lantern, *M'mselle*," he said.

She saw it was a simply-made one of a candle in a jam-jar.

She thought they would at least be able to see their way if they were going into a cave.

At the same time, she was frightened.

It was bad enough that Sardos had taken the *Duc* prisoner.

If he also captured her and Pierre, he might either kill them too, or use them as hostages.

However, there was no point in arguing.

She merely followed Pierre out of the front-door and down the small garden.

It was light outside because the moon was rising.

The stars were already brilliant in the sable sky.

Pierre turned sharply to the right and ran to where the rocks sloped down onto the field.

Marcia had no time to think.

She was concerned only with keeping up with Pierre.

She was also holding up her nightdress and *négligée* so that she could run quicker.

She was fortunately still wearing the heel-less satin slippers she had worn for dinner.

Aquilin was still in the field.

She guessed that Sardos and his accomplices had captured the *Duc* before he was able to reach his horse.

Suddenly Pierre stopped.

As Marcia reached him he whispered:

"There's the cave into which they took the *Duc*!"

He pointed.

Marcia could see vaguely the faint outline of what might be an entrance to a cave.

She would have moved towards it to see if she could hear anything, but Pierre caught hold of her arm and pulled her away.

They moved on about three yards, and Pierre stopped again.

Now Marcia could see a small opening in the rock which looked as if it might have been used by an animal.

Pierre pulled his lantern, as he called it, from out of his coat, where he was hiding it.

In a whisper she could hardly hear him saying:

"Follow me!"

He crawled into the hole ahead of them on hands and knees, and Marcia did the same.

She felt encumbered by her nightclothes round her knees.

It was a relief when, after moving for only a short distance, Pierre stood up.

He held his lantern so that she could see that they were in a small but empty chamber and that the roof above them was rough and stony.

It was high enough, however, for them to be able to stand up straight.

Pierre put his finger to his lips to tell her to be silent.

Marcia was already aware that if they spoke, their voices would echo and alert Sardos.

Pierre went ahead, moving slowly because the floor was uneven.

Now Marcia could see in the flickering light that there were stalactites hanging from the roof as well as stalagmites rising from the floor.

They moved farther on.

Now they were no longer in a cave, but in what seemed like a very narrow passage.

Pierre was holding the lantern so that it gave Marcia enough light to follow him.

Its glow was hidden from in front by his coat which he held over it.

It was then she heard a voice in the distance.

Whoever was speaking was doing so quietly.

Nevertheless, his voice echoed eerily, so that it seemed as if it came from another Planet.

Pierre walked on and Marcia followed, stumbling occasionally on the rough rocks.

She steadied herself by putting out her hands so that she could touch the walls on either side.

They were very cold.

She realised that the farther they went, the colder it was.

Then suddenly she heard Sardos's voice quite near her say roughly:

"Tighten those knots so that he cannot escape!"

Pierre had stopped when he heard Sardos.

Now he moved forward very, very slowly, on tip-toe.

There was the sound of some-one being dragged over rough ground.

Then, as Marcia moved round a rough projection of rock, she realised she could look through a large crack into what was an amazing cave.

It was so high that it was impossible in the darkness to see the top of it.

Inside there were what looked like huge trees of sta-lagmites which glistened and glittered in the light from a large lantern.

The lantern was standing on a rock which was flat and almost the size of a table.

It illuminated the four men in the cave.

To the left of her, Marcia could see Sardos looking, she thought, extremely unpleasant and aggressive.

Just in front was the *Duc*.

He was bare-headed and there was a gash on his cheek where he must have been struck.

His coat had been pulled off one shoulder and the upper part of his body was encircled by a rope.

Just beyond him she could see an enormous man, coarse and common in appearance.

She would not have been surprised if she was told he was a Pugilist.

There was another man there who looked small and insignificant beside the man who was holding the *Duc* prisoner.

He was grey-headed and had a crafty look about him which made Marcia feel that no-one with any sense would trust him.

The big man pulled the *Duc* up against the rock which held the lantern.

It was then Marcia saw the third man draw some papers from his pocket.

He placed them on the flat rock in front of him.

Then she heard the *Duc* speak.

"I suppose, Sardos," he said, "you know what you are doing, and that I deeply resent the way in which I am being treated."

"You may resent it," Sardos replied in a rude voice, "but I resent the way you are so close-fisted with your money, and I have no intention of going to Prison when you can so easily pay my Debts."

"As I have done in the past," the *Duc* said quietly.

"And which there will be no need for you to do in the future!"

"So you intend to kill me," the *Duc* remarked in a calm voice.

"That will be up to you," Sardos replied, "and you have a choice."

There was silence. The *Duc* waited.

Watching him, and Marcia could see his face in profile, she thought he was very calm and brave.

He must be aware of the perilous position he was in.

Quite suddenly Sardos laughed, and it was an evil sound.

"It rather turns the tables, does it not, Uncle Armond," he said, "with me dictating the terms rather than you."

"I am waiting to learn," the *Duc* replied, "what those terms are."

"Very well," Sardos answered. "You shall hear them and that is why I have brought you to this delightful cave."

"I had no idea it existed," the *Duc* replied.

"You can thank Albert here for that," Sardos said. "When he showed it to me, I knew it was exactly what I wanted."

"To keep me prisoner?" the *Duc* enquired.

"That is up to you," Sardos said, "but let me first introduce you to my friends—Albert, it may not surprise you to hear, is the strongest man in Bergerac, and has a great number of fights and wrestling-matches to his credit."

He gave another of his unpleasant laughs as he added:

"I advise you not to fight him, as you would undoubtedly be the loser."

The *Duc* did not speak, and Marcia thought he was marvellously self-controlled.

At the same time, she could just see a little pulse beating in his neck.

It told her he was, in fact, very angry.

"My other friend, *Monsieur* Luzech is, as you might guess, a Solicitor. He has here some papers for you to sign, which you would be very foolish not to do."

"May I know what those papers contain?" the *Duc* enquired.

"They name me as your Heir unless you have a son," Sardos said, his voice rising, "but first you will give me the sum of two-million *francs* and make over to me all the property you own in Bergerac."

Listening, Marcia knew that Bergerac was a large

town only a few miles from the *Château*.

If the *Duc* had valuable freehold property there, the rents probably brought him in a great deal of the money he spent on his relatives and on his Estate.

She was not surprised when the *Duc* refused.

"And if I refuse to sign this monstrous document?"

"Then, my dear Uncle," Sardos answered, "I shall most regretfully, and of course, it will cause me deep distress, leave you here in this beautiful, if somewhat chilly, cave. It had never been discovered until Albert was clever enough to find it, and just the movement of a few rocks at the entrance will leave it undiscovered for another thousand years which it has already spent unnoticed."

There was silence as his voice and its attendant echo died away.

"So my Aunt the *Comtesse* was right in saying you were planning to murder me!" the *Duc* remarked.

"Why should she have said that?" Sardos asked angrily.

"She heard that you were asserting in Paris that my death would be quite soon. So if I should disappear now without any explanation, you will find a great number of people will wish to ask you questions as to when you last saw me."

Marcia thought this was clever of the *Duc*.

She could see by the expression on Sardos's face that he was disconcerted.

"Nevertheless," he said, "there is no need for there to be any risks. You will sign these papers, which are entirely legal, and *Monsieur* Luzech will have them registered immediately so that it will be impossible for you to go back on your word."

"Very well," the *Duc* said. "But I am sure you realise

that it would be impossible for me to sign anything, tied up as I am. I am quite incapable of using my hands."

Sardos drew a revolver from his pocket and pointed it at the *Duc*.

"Untie him, Albert!" he ordered. "And make sure you also have your revolver ready. If he tries to escape, shoot him!"

The huge man standing beside the *Duc* began to unknot the rope by which he was bound.

Marcia was afraid that the *Duc* was going to take the risk of fighting for his liberty.

She knew it would prove disastrous.

There were two revolvers pointed at him.

While she might be able to shoot one man, she was quite certain if she did so that either Sardos or Albert would kill the *Duc*.

The rope fell to the ground and the *Duc* shook his hands as if to bring the blood back into them.

"Are the papers ready?" Sardos asked the Solicitor.

"They are here and in order, exactly as you requested, *Monsieur*," he replied in a slimy voice.

Marcia was sure he was being well paid for his pains.

She thought he seemed to relish the sight of the *Duc* in the humiliating position in which he stood.

"Come over here, Uncle Armond," Sardos said sharply. "And no tricks or you die!"

The *Duc* took a step forward.

As he did so, Marcia lifted her revolver and brought it down on the lantern.

The report was shattering as it echoed and re-echoed round the cave.

Then in the darkness she reached out and caught the *Duc* by the hand.

She pulled him, as Sardos shouted in fury, to the slit

in the rocks through which she had been looking.

Without speaking, she dragged at his hand and he real-ised that he could just get through the gap, although it was difficult and somewhat painful.

Only when he was out of the big cave and beside her did Marcia whisper:

"Pierre can get us out."

The boy was intelligent enough to shield the back of his candle-lantern in his coat as he had done before.

It threw just a little light ahead of him so that Marcia and the *Duc* could follow him.

Behind them the noise was deafening.

"Shoot him!" Sardos was shouting. "Shoot him! He is escaping!"

He fired his revolver.

There was a scream of pain, then there was the echo of the explosion.

Marcia thought he must have hit Albert.

There was another shot and yet another, then a sound of stones crashing to the ground.

It might have been stalagmites collapsing or it might have been stones falling from the roof.

The only thing Marcia wanted was to get the *Duc* away as quickly as possible.

She feared that Sardos would pursue him and capture him again.

Pierre moved quickly.

When they were well away from the big cave, the boy held his small lantern high.

They were then able to follow him more easily.

It took only a few minutes, but it seemed to Marcia more like several hours before they reached the entrance.

Pierre went down on his knees and the *Duc* waited for her to follow before he did the same.

It seemed very warm outside.

The moonlight made it easy for them to climb over the rocks at the foot of the gorge.

When they had reached familiar ground, Marcia said:

"You must get away at once! *Aquilin* is there waiting for you."

"And leave you behind?" the *Duc* asked.

"They are not concerned with me," Marcia replied.

"They might be," he insisted.

It was then that Pierre, who was extinguishing his precious lantern, gave a cry.

"It's *Maman*," he said. "*Maman*'s home!"

Without waiting for anyone to reply, he ran off.

Marcia, looking towards the little cottage, saw there was a cart outside it.

It was a rough cart such as the Carriers in that part of the country used to transport their wares from the villages to the Market Towns.

"If Lisette's Mother is home, I can come back with you, *Monsieur,*" Marcia said.

She did not wait for the *Duc* to answer, but ran after Pierre.

His Mother was already inside the house.

He had flung his arms round the neck of a woman with a kind, rather tired face.

"You're back, *Maman!* You're back!" he was saying. "Some terrible things have been happening!"

"What is wrong?" his Mother asked.

She looked in astonishment as Marcia came down the path and into the house.

"I am afraid Lisette has had an accident," Marcia explained. "I was riding one of *Monsieur le Duc*'s horses and jumped a hedge just near your home without being aware that Lisette was picking flowers on the other side of it."

She saw the woman go very pale and added quickly:

"She is unconscious, but we think it is only a slight concussion. She is in the bed-room."

As Marcia spoke, Lisette's Mother opened the bed-room door and went in.

She ran to the bed, and as she bent over her child, Lisette gave a little cry.

"*Maman! Maman!* I'se hurt!"

Her Mother sat down on the bed and held her very closely against her breast.

"She is conscious!" Marcia exclaimed. "And she has spoken, that means that her brain is undamaged. Oh, I am glad . . . so very . . . glad!"

Her voice broke on the words.

The *Duc,* coming into the room behind her, saw the tears in her eyes.

Holding Lisette closely in her arms, her Mother looked with amazement at the *Duc.*

When she would have risen, the *Duc* said:

"Do not move. I can only say how sorry I am that this has happened. I can also tell you that I owe a great debt of gratitude to your son, who has saved my life."

"Saved your life, *Monsieur?*" the woman murmured.

"There is no time to tell you about it now," the *Duc* said, "as I must take Lady Marcia, who has been taking care of Lisette, back to the *Château.* I will call on you some time to-morrow, and I promise you that because of what Pierre has done for me, you will all be very much more comfortable in the future."

Pierre's Mother was too surprised to say anything.

Lisette was murmuring: "*Maman, Maman!*" ·
her.

The *Duc* put out his hand to Marcia.

"Come along," he said. "We must take *Aquilin* to his stables. Jacques can collect your things tomorrow."

Marcia wiped the tears from her eyes, and without saying anything went from the room.

Pierre was standing in the small passage.

The *Duc* put his hand on his shoulder.

"Thanks to you, Pierre," he said, "I have escaped from those men, who had no right to behave as they did. Look after your Mother and buy something nice in the village. I will talk to you later about your future."

He gave the boy two golden *louis* as he spoke.

Pierre stared at them, unable to speak.

The *Duc* drew Marcia out of the house and across the garden into the field.

He gave a low whistle and *Aquilin* came trotting towards him.

"The sooner we get away," the *Duc* said, "the better!"

He lifted Marcia onto the saddle and sprang up behind her.

Putting his left arm round her, he held the reins with his other hand.

Marcia held her breath until they were away from the cottage and had passed the entrance to the cave.

She was terrified in case she saw Sardos and Albert coming out.

They might fire at the *Duc* as they rode past.

She knew the *Duc* was thinking the same thing.

But while he made *Aquilin* move quickly, he did not allow him to break into a gallop.

It was because he knew this would be uncomfortable for Marcia.

She thought that no other man in the same circumstances would think of her rather than of himself.

A few minutes later they had left danger behind.

They were now moving quickly in the moonlight, and Marcia could see the *Château* ahead of them.

Only as they drew near to the stables did she realise that to arrive wearing only her night-attire would cause comment.

As they drew still nearer, she said quickly:

"Perhaps I had better walk the rest of the way. If anyone sees me, they will think it very strange."

"I am aware of that," the *Duc* said briefly.

Instead of going directly to the stables, he moved through some trees and shrubs.

It brought them to the gardens at the back of the *Château*.

He drew in *Aquilin* and said to Marcia:

"If you wait here, I will take you in through a door where no-one will see you. But first I must put *Aquilin* in his stall."

"Yes, of course." She smiled.

She slipped from the saddle down onto the ground, and the *Duc* rode off.

When she was alone, Marcia found herself saying a prayer of thankfulness that she had been able to rescue him.

She knew now that Sardos had been inspecting the cave when she saw him coming from that direction.

The man accompanying him must have been Albert.

"How can he have thought of anything so wicked?" she asked herself.

Then, of course, the next question was:

"How soon will he try again?"

She was quite sure he would not give up easily.

He needed money desperately.

Though the *Duc* had not died to-night, there was every likelihood of his doing so in the near future.

"How can he possibly live in such circumstances?" she asked herself.

She was so deep in her thoughts that she was startled when suddenly she found the *Duc* beside her.

"*Aquilin* has gone to bed," he said, "and the sooner you do the same thing, the better! You have had enough shocks for one day!"

"I was just thanking God that I was able to save you," Marcia said. "But . . . suppose he . . . tries . . . again?"

"Then we must be ready for him," the *Duc* replied quietly.

As if he thought it was a mistake to talk about it, he took Marcia by the hand.

He drew her across the garden towards the house.

The whole place seemed to be in darkness, and the house was very quiet.

Marcia hoped that everybody had gone to bed.

She had no wish to encounter the *Comtesse* or, for that matter, her Father.

The *Duc* opened a window on the Ground Floor where the catch had been broken and not yet repaired.

She thought it was unlike him to have anything that was not perfect about his house.

But in this instance it was a blessing rather than an error.

The *Duc* lifted her over the sill.

She found herself in a small room which she suspected was not much used.

Outside in the corridor the staircase was only sparingly lit.

On the first floor, lights were still burning in the sconces which bore the *Duc*'s arms.

When they reached her bed-room he took one of the candles to light a candle-stick beside her bed.

She was aware that she was not expected, because otherwise the candles would have been left burning.

She guessed then that Jacques had told the maid that she was staying with friends.

The *Duc,* having finished lighting three candles, blew out the one he held in his hand.

"We are home and . . . you are . . . safe!" Marcia said. "At least . . . for the . . . moment."

"And I have you to thank for saving me," the *Duc* said quietly.

"You will have to be careful . . . very careful!" Marcia warned.

She looked up at him, her hair gleaming golden in the candlelight.

Her eyes were anxious because she was worried that Sardos would strike again.

The *Duc* put his arms round her and pulled her against him.

As Marcia gave a little gasp of surprise, his lips came down on hers.

He kissed her gently, as if he were thanking her for what she had done for him.

Then his kiss became demanding and possessive.

Marcia at first was unable to realise what was happening.

Then something stirred in her breast which seemed to be part of the moonlight and which moved upwards until it reached her lips.

It was then the *Duc* raised his head.

"How can you make me feel like this?" he asked.

Then he was kissing her again, kissing her so that she felt as if the whole *Château* swung round her.

The stars seemed to fall from the sky and the moonlight streaked through her body as if it were lightning.

147

It was so rapturous, so unlike anything she had ever experienced before, she could not believe it was really happening.

Finally the *Duc* set her free.

"Go to bed," he said in a voice that was unrecognisable. "We will talk about this in the morning."

Marcia swayed because he had taken his arms from her.

He picked her up and laid her on the bed.

As her head touched the pillow he kissed her once more.

It was a long, passionate kiss which drew her heart from her body and made it his.

Then before she could speak he was gone and the door had shut behind him.

Marcia lay back, thinking that the whole world had turned topsy-turvy.

There was nothing left but the throbbing of her heart.

* * *

Marcia woke and was aware that somebody was in her room.

She thought it must be her Father, but whoever it was had pulled back the curtains and the sunshine had flooded in.

To her astonishment, she saw that it was the *Duc* who stood there.

He came towards her from the window and sat down on the side of the bed, facing her.

"You look very lovely in the morning!" he said.

"What has . . . happened? Why are you . . . here?" Marcia asked.

She felt the terror of last night returning.

"It is not . . . Sardos?"

"It is not Sardos at the moment," the *Duc* said quietly, "but you know as well as I do that he will try to kill me again."

"Oh . . . no . . . no!" Marcia exclaimed.

She sat up in bed, her golden hair falling over her shoulders.

The diaphanous nightgown she wore outlined the perfect curves of her breasts.

"You must go away!" she said quickly. "You have to be . . . protected until there is . . . something we can do . . . about him."

"I will not run away," the *Duc* said quietly, "but I have decided what I must do, and I need your help."

"You know I will . . . help you in . . . any way if . . . I can," Marcia replied. "What is . . . it?"

"The only way I can save myself and also what is more important, the Family name and the Estate, is to be married," the *Duc* said. "I am therefore asking you, Marcia, to save my life by marrying me this morning in my Private Chapel here in the *Château*."

He paused.

Marcia did not speak, but her eyes seemed to fill her whole face.

"The alternative," he went on, "is that I can make you mine here and now, and any child born of our union will be my legitimate Heir, replacing Sardos."

"Can you . . . really be . . . saying that . . . to me?" Marcia asked.

"It is something I have no wish to say," the *Duc* answered, "but I am desperate. And if I am to save my Family, who would starve with Sardos in my place, that is what I will do. I also have an obligation to the people on the Estate."

He looked into Marcia's eyes before he said very gently:

"Before you answer me, I should tell you that I love you! That is something I have never before said to any woman, and I have never before wanted to marry any woman. If you will marry me, Marcia, I swear it is what I want with all my heart and with my eternal soul."

He drew a deep breath before he asked:

"Will you save me?"

Marcia smiled.

"It is not . . . difficult for me to . . . give you my answer for . . . I love you too! I knew . . . last night when you . . . kissed me why I had been so . . . worried about you, and why I had to . . . save you. It was because I had . . . fallen . . . in love!"

"That makes two of us!" the *Duc* said softly.

He bent forward and his lips found Marcia's.

He kissed her gently and tenderly as if she was very precious.

"I have already sent for my Chaplain," he said. "If we are married at noon, no-one in the house will know about our wedding until you are my wife."

Marcia clasped her hands together.

"Can we really do that? I could not bear to have them . . . talking and speculating! And Papa and the *Comtesse* will say how clever they were to have brought us together."

"We will not say anything about Sardos until after you are my wife," the *Duc* replied, "and I will be responsible for what we have done, or not done. I will certainly not allow anyone to bully you!"

Marcia laughed.

"That is what *you* are doing, and I love it! It is what I want you to do. Oh, Armond, how can this have happened so . . . surprisingly?"

He moved his lips over the softness of her cheek before he said:

"It is not really surprising. I knew when you walked into the *Salon* that you were not only the most beautiful woman I had ever seen, but that you were an angel come down from Heaven about to change my life, even though I fought against it happening."

"You were very rude and very disagreeable!" Marcia protested.

"It is something I will make up for in the future," the *Duc* answered.

He kissed her again before he said:

"I am going now to make arrangements. It would be a mistake for anyone to find me here until my ring is on your finger."

"I think it is a bit late to worry about my reputation," Marcia remarked, "but tell me, please, before you go— what are you going to do . . . about those . . . horrible men?"

"I had a feeling when they were firing off their pistols," the *Duc* replied, "that because it was indiscriminate it might have dislodged some of the rocks. It is possible they will be unable to escape until they are rescued."

Marcia gave a little cry.

"Do you really . . . think that is . . . true?"

"I suppose I must behave like a gentleman and rescue them," the *Duc* observed, "before they die of starvation. But I cannot help feeling it would be a blessing to the world if they were left to remain where they are."

"I agree with you," Marcia said. "At the same time, it would be . . . wrong."

"I know," the *Duc* replied, "and later this afternoon I will send some of my men to find out what has happened."

"You will . . . not go with . . . them?"

The *Duc* shook his head.

"No, I think that would be a mistake. Besides, I want to be with you. My Estate Manager, who is a very intelligent man, will be in charge of the rescue operations."

Marcia shuddered.

She could not help feeling that once Sardos was free, he would be thinking up other ways of destroying the *Duc*.

As if he knew what she was thinking, the *Duc* put his fingers under her chin and turned her face up to his.

"I am going to make you my wife, my darling, and once we are married you can look after me as you have done already. Perhaps God will be merciful and find some way of keeping us safe."

Impulsively Marcia put her arms around his neck.

"I love you! I love you!" she cried. "How can I . . . lose you?"

He kissed her before he said:

"This is our Wedding-Day and nothing must disturb our happiness. I will leave you now, my precious wife-to-be. When my ring is on your finger I will show you how much you mean to me."

He kissed her again, and she saw the love in his eyes.

She knew then that this was what she had wanted and what she had waited for.

When the *Duc* left her, she rang for the maid.

Because she did not wish to face the *Comtesse* or any of the other members of the house-party, she had her breakfast in bed.

It was eleven o'clock. She was thinking she should get dressed, when Jacques knocked on her door.

He brought her a veil which he told her had been in the Roux Family for two centuries.

He also handed her a wreath of orange-blossom made in diamonds.

It was unique and very beautiful.

Marcia hid it from her lady's-maid until the last minute.

First, to the maid's surprise, she put on a very beautiful gown of white chiffon and lace.

She had worn it at a State Ball at Buckingham Palace.

The veil went over her hair and the orange-blossom wreath held it in place on her head.

She knew when she looked in the mirror that the *Duc* would not be ashamed of his English Bride.

"Please, do not say a word to anybody until after we are married," she begged the maid.

"*Mais non, M'mselle!* It's so exciting! May *le Bon Dieu* bless you and *Monsieur le Duc!*"

"He has blessed us already," Marcia said softly.

The *Duc* came into the *Boudoir* looking magnificent in his evening-dress—the correct wear in France for a Bridegroom.

His coat was covered with decorations, and there was another on a ribbon round his neck.

As Marcia advanced towards him, he did not move, but only watched her until she reached him.

There was an expression on his face which she had never seen before.

She knew it was Love, the Love she had sought but believed she would never find.

She thought of the Nurseries upstairs and knew that their children would be born of Love.

If God was merciful and the *Duc* survived, there would never be anyone else in either of their lives.

The *Duc* gave her a small bouquet made of white orchids.

Then he kissed her hand before taking her arm and leading her from the *Boudoir*.

To reach the Chapel they went down the same side staircase that they had climbed last night.

The *Duc*'s Chaplain was waiting for them.

Marcia saw that the altar was amassed with lilies and the same white orchids that comprised her bouquet.

She felt she could read the *Duc*'s mind.

He was saying to her with flowers that she was everything he wanted as his wife, that she was different from any other woman who had amused him but whom he had always found somehow disappointing.

The Service was begun.

Because it was also a Mass, there were two Servers, and Marcia recognised one of them as being Pierre.

She knew there was nothing that could have given the boy more pleasure.

The village would be gratified when it was known he had actually been present at the *Duc*'s marriage.

Because the *Duc* was so wonderful, he had known how the boy would feel.

It was a quality she had always wanted in her husband.

Her fingers tightened on his, and he knew by the expression in her eyes that she understood.

When the Chaplain blessed them, it seemed to Marcia that the angels were singing overhead.

The light of the Divine enveloped them both.

When they rose to their feet the *Duc* kissed her gently before they went down the short aisle and out of the Chapel.

"Now, my precious," he said, "I am afraid we have to face the music, but I do not want you to be upset."

"Nothing can upset me now that I am your wife," Marcia said. "Oh, darling, did you pray, as I did, that we could have a long Honeymoon?"

"I prayed that God would be merciful and not punish me for my sins," the *Duc* answered.

He looked at her for a moment before he said:

"I love you and I want you! Let us get all the congratulations over, then we can be alone."

"That is . . . what I . . . want," Marcia answered.

He drew her from the Chapel down the long corridor which led them towards the *Salon d'Or*.

She could hear voices and looked enquiringly at the *Duc*.

"I told everybody to wait for me here, as I had an announcement to make," he explained.

"I hope they will not be angry that they were left out of the Wedding-Service," Marcia said.

"Let them," the *Duc* replied. "No-one can upset us now."

Marcia thought he was tempting Fate by saying something like that.

She quickly said a prayer that Sardos would not appear.

The *Major Domo* was waiting in the Hall ready to open the *Salon* door.

"Announce us," the *Duc* ordered, "as man and wife!"

In a stentorian voice the *Major Domo* obliged.

"Monsieur le Duc et Madame la Duchesse de Roux!"

There was an astonished silence from the party gathered in the *Salon*.

Then, as they saw how Marcia and the *Duc* were dressed, there were shrieks of excitement.

It was the *Comtesse* who reached them first.

"You have been married!" she exclaimed. "I do not believe it! How can you have done this without telling me!"

"That is a story you will hear later," the *Duc* said firmly.

Marcia had run to her Father.

"This is a surprise!" the Earl exclaimed.

"I know, Papa," Marcia replied, "and I will tell you all about it later, but not here . . . not in front of all these people."

The Earl, however, was so delighted that his daughter had done exactly what he wanted that he was not really curious about the details.

All he wanted was to toast them and wish them happiness for ever.

Everybody seemed to want to make a speech until they went into the Dining-Room for luncheon.

Afterwards the *Duc* and Marcia escaped upstairs.

Marcia found when she went into her bed-room that on the *Duc*'s instructions the room had been decorated with white flowers.

Her *Boudoir* had also been decorated with them, but she had eyes only for her husband.

"I love you so wildly," he said, "that I cannot believe this has all happened so quickly. My Darling, I will be very gentle with you, and you must prevent me from frightening or hurting you."

"I love you . . . I love you so . . . much," Marcia answered, "and I know that only God could have brought us . . . together and made it possible for us to find . . . the love we were both seeking."

"That is true," the *Duc* agreed.

Then he was kissing her until there were no difficulties, no horrors, no fear.

There was only Love—Love—Love!

As the *Duc* made Marcia his, they entered a Heaven that was all their own.

It was late in the evening.

The *Duc* was giving orders to Jacques that he and Marcia would dine in the *Boudoir*.

"We will wait on ourselves," he said, "and make it clear to everybody that we do not wish to be disturbed."

"I'll see to it, *Monsieur*," Jacques answered.

He was thinking, as he spoke, that he had never seen his Master look so happy.

"There is, however, one person who would like to speak to you first, *Monsieur*," he said aloud.

"Who is it?" the *Duc* asked impatiently.

"The Manager you sent to the cave," Jacques answered. "He came back half-an-hour ago and is waiting to speak to you, *Monsieur,* when it is convenient."

It was not convenient. He had no wish to think of anybody but Marcia.

But the *Duc* thought that if he did not see the man, he would be wondering what they had found.

"Send him in, Jacques," he said resignedly.

He walked back into the bed-room, where Marcia was lying under the canopy of the huge bed.

She was surrounded by orchids and lilies and looking very much like a lily herself.

The *Duc* sat down on the side of the bed.

"My Manager is back," he said. "I sent him, as I told you I would, to dig Sardos and those men out."

"Yes, of course . . . you were . . . right," she said in a low voice. "But . . . oh, Darling . . . you do not think that . . . Sardos will come . . . here?"

"I am quite certain he will do nothing like that," the *Duc* answered. "He is free, at least for the moment, and like an animal he will slink away to lick his wounds."

There was a harsh note in the *Duc*'s voice which Marcia did not miss.

"Then let us hear the worst," she said, "and I hope he has gone to . . . Paris!"

The *Duc* kissed her.

"Try not to worry, my precious one," he said.

"I am thinking only of you," Marcia whispered.

"That is exactly what I was going to say to you," he answered.

He went back into the *Boudoir* and told Jacques to send in the Manager.

The man, who had been in the *Duc*'s employment for nearly ten years, was very competent.

He came into the room.

"What has happened?" the *Duc* asked.

"I'm afraid I've got bad news," the Manager replied.

"What is it?" the *Duc* asked quickly.

"It was as you thought, *Monsieur*. The rocks had fallen across the entrance, which prevented those inside from escaping. It took some time for us to remove them, and when we did we found the three men, including the *Comte* de Thiviers, just as you expected."

"They were alive?"

"Non, Monsieur!"

"Dead—all dead?" the *Duc* exclaimed.

"The *Comte* and a large man who looked like a Pugilist were both shot."

"Shot?" the *Duc* exclaimed.

"It looked, *Monsieur,* as if each of them shot the other simultaneously. Both men had revolvers still in their hands."

The *Duc* drew in his breath.

"And the third man?"

"He too is dead, *Monsieur,* but I think from fright and from the cold."

The *Duc* was silent.

It was a most convenient ending to what had been a very difficult and perilous situation.

The Manager waited.

At last the *Duc* ordered:

"Have the body of the *Comte* de Thiviers taken to the crypt of the Chapel, and arrange for the burial to take place quietly and, if possible, without the newspapers getting to hear of it."

"*Oui, Monsieur,* I understand," the Manager replied.

"The other men should be buried in the Cemetery in Bergerac. I feel sure the Doctor can arrange that."

"I will see to it, *Monsieur le Duc,*" the Manager said.

"Thank you," the *Duc* replied. "I am very grateful."

The Manager paused. Then he said:

"May I wish you, *Monsieur le Duc*, and *Madame la Duchesse* every happiness. We are all very thrilled and delighted that you are married!"

"It took place very quietly," the *Duc* said, "but you can tell everybody on the Estate that we intend to celebrate in the usual way with a feast and fireworks in three or four weeks' time, when we come back from our Honeymoon. I know I can leave it to you to make all the arrangements."

"*Certainement,*" the Manager said, "and it will be something very exciting for everybody to look forward to."

* * *

The *Duc* walked back from the *Boudoir.*

Marcia was not in bed, but standing waiting for him by the window.

As he entered the room she ran towards him and cried:

"What has . . . happened? Is everything all right? Oh, Darling . . . Darling, you are . . . not in . . . danger?"

The *Duc* put his arms around her.

"Our prayers have been answered," he said, "and now we can live the life we both want without fear and without anybody trying to hurt us."

"Is that . . . really true? Is Sardos . . . dead?"

"He is! That man Albert must have shot him!"

"Oh, Armond . . . I was so frightened for . . . you!"

The tears were running down Marcia's cheeks as she clung to the *Duc*.

They were tears of happiness, and he felt like crying himself because he was so grateful and so thankful.

He could love Marcia the way he wanted to without being afraid for them both every time a door opened.

"Thank you, God," the *Duc* said in his heart as Marcia was saying in hers.

Then they were kissing each other wildly, fiercely, and passionately, as if they had both come back from the grave.

They knew, in fact, that this was the beginning of a new life.

It was a life in which their children would be surrounded by a Love that was pure and perfect and came from God.

ABOUT THE AUTHOR

BARBARA CARTLAND, the world's most famous romantic novelist, who is also an historian, play-wright, lecturer, political speaker and television personality, has now written over 558 books and sold over 600 million copies all over the world.

She has also had many historical works published and has written four autobiographies as well as the biographies of her mother and that of her brother, Ronald Cartland, who was the first Member of Parliament to be killed in the last war. This book has a preface by Sir Winston Churchill and has just been republished with an introduction by Sir Arthur Bryant.

Love at the Helm, a novel written with the help and inspiration of the late Earl Mountbatten of Burma, Great Uncle of His Royal Highness The Prince of Wales, is being sold for the Mountbatten Memorial Trust.

She has broken the world record for the last sixteen years by writing an average of twenty-three books a year. In the *Guinness Book of Records* she is listed as the world's top-selling author.

Miss Cartland in 1978 sang an Album of Love Songs with the Royal Philharmonic Orchestra.

In private life Barbara Cartland, who is a Dame of the Order of St. John of Jerusalem, Chairman of the St. John Council in Hertfordshire and Deputy President of the St. John Ambulance Brigade, has fought for better conditions and salaries for Midwives and Nurses.

She championed the cause for the Elderly in 1956, invoking a Government Enquiry into the "Housing Conditions of Old People."

In 1962 she had the Law of England changed so that Local Authorities had to provide camps for their own Gypsies. This has meant that since then thousands and thousands of Gypsy children have been able to go to School, which they had never been able to do in the past, as their caravans were moved every twenty-four hours by the Police.

There are now fourteen camps in Hertfordshire and Barbara Cartland has her own Romany Gypsy Camp, called Barbaraville by the Gypsies.

Her designs "Decorating with Love" are being sold all over the U.S.A. and the National Home Fashions League made her, in 1981, "Woman of Achievement."

She is unique in that she was one and two in the Dalton list of Best Sellers, and one week had four books in the top twenty.

Barbara Cartland's book *Getting Older, Growing Younger* has been published in Great Britain and the U.S.A. and her fifth cookery book, *The Romance of Food,* is now being used by the House of Commons.

In 1984 she received at Kennedy Airport America's Bishop Wright Air Industry Award for her contribution to the development of aviation. In 1931 she and two R.A.F. Officers thought of, and carried, the first aeroplane-towed glider airmail.

During the war she was Chief Lady Welfare Officer in Bedfordshire, looking after 20,000 Service men and women. She thought of having a pool of Wedding Dresses at the War Office so a Service Bride could hire a gown for the day.

She bought 1,000 gowns without coupons for the A.T.S., the W.A.A.F.'s and the W.R.E.N.S. In 1945 Barbara Cartland received the Certificate of Merit from Eastern Command.

In 1964 Barbara Cartland founded the National Association for Health of which she is the President, as a front for all the Health Stores and for any product made as alternative medicine.

This is now a £65 million turnover a year, with one-third going in export.

In January 1988 she received *La Médaille de Vermeil de la Ville de Paris*. This is the highest award to be given in France by the City of Paris. She has sold 25 million books in France.

In March 1988 Barbara Cartland was asked by the Indian Government to open their Health Resort outside Delhi. This is almost the largest Health Resort in the world.

Barbara Cartland was received with great enthusiasm by her fans, who fêted her at a reception in the City, and she received the gift of an embossed plate from the Government.

Barbara Cartland was made a Dame of the Order of the British Empire in the 1991 New Year's Honours List by Her Majesty, The Queen, for her contribution to Literature and also for her years of work for the community.

Called after her own beloved Camfield Place, each Camfield Novel of Love by Barbara Cartland is a thrilling, never-before published love story by the greatest romance writer of all time.

Barbara Cartland